QUEST FOR KOLDER

Somewhere the not-quite-human invaders from the place called Kolder were holed up, waiting for the chance to resume their conquest of a world. Somewhere they were storing up the super-science of an adjoining world against the hour of their new assault.

Simon Tregarth knew he and his princess wife would know no peace until the last had been heard of Kolder. His task was twofold: track down its lair, then smash the gateway.

Yet the only way to start this counterattack would be by first allowing himself—and perhaps his loved one—to fall into Kolder's monstrous hands.

WEB OF THE WITCH WORLD combines the best of science-fiction with the most colorful heroic fantasy.

ANDRE NORTON
WEB OF THE WITCH WORLD

ace books
A Division of Charter Communications Inc.
A GROSSET & DUNLAP COMPANY
360 Park Avenue South
New York, New York 10010

1 GAUNTLET THROWN

In the night there had been storm with great gusts of angry wind to batter ancient walls, aim spear-thrusts of rain at the window slits of the chamber. But its violence had been reduced to a sullen mutter outside the South Keep. And Simon Tregarth had found that mutter soothing.

No, this was no troubling of nature—the raw nature men must fight and subdue for his own survival. It was a very different unease he felt as he lay in the early morning, awake and aware as a sentinel listening to sounds beyond his post.

Chill sweat gathered in his armpits, beaded dankly on his slightly hollowed cheeks and square jaw. Gray light overtook the room shadows, there was no sound, but—

His hand went out tentatively before he consciously thought. Nor did he entirely realize that he was yielding to an emotion which he still found new and hard to understand. This was an instinctive appeal for comradeship and support against—what? He could set no name to the uneasiness which held him.

Fingers met warm flesh, cupped on soft skin. He turned his head on the pillow. The lamp was unlit, but

5

there was wan light enough to see his bedfellow. Open, watchful eyes met his fearlessly, but their depths were shadowed by a twin to the anxiety growing in Simon.

Then she moved. Jaelithe, she who had been a witch of Estcarp, and was now his wife, sat up abruptly, the black silk of her hair pulling from beneath his cheek to cloak her shoulders, her hands folded over her small high breasts. She no longer gazed at him, but searched the room, open to their sight since the midsummer mildness had led to the bed hangings being looped up for the free passage of night breezes.

The strangeness of that chamber came and went for Simon. Sometimes the present was a dream, ill-rooted and illusory, when he thought of the past. At other times it was the past which had no part of him at all. What was he? Simon Tregarth—disgraced ex-army officer, a criminal who had fled the vengeance of wolves beyond the law, who had taken the final step of the perfect escape known to that evil world—the "gate." Jorge Petronius had opened it for him—an age-old stone seat rumored to take any man daring enough to sit in it to a new world, one where his talents would make him at home. That was one Simon Tregarth.

Another lay here and now in the South Keep of Estcarp, March Warder of the south, sworn to the service of the Women of Power; he had taken to wife one of the feared witches of the age-sombered land of Estcarp. And this was one of the times when the present annulled the past—when he crossed a border he could not describe into a firmer union with the world he had so abruptly entered.

Sharp as any sword thrust into his flesh was that throb, breaking through his momentary wonder concerning himself and what he was doing here. He moved as quickly as Jaelithe had earlier, sitting up so that their shoulders brushed, and in his hand was a dart gun. But even as Simon brought that out from under his pillow, he knew the folly of his action. This was not a call to battle, but a clarion summons far more subtle and, in its way, more terrifying.

"Simon—" Jaelithe's voice was shaken, higher than usual and a little unsteady.

"I know!" He was already sliding over the edge of the wide bed, his feet meeting the first step of the dais which supported it above the floor of the chamber, his hands reaching for the garments left on the chair beyond.

Somewhere—either in the pile of the South Keep or near thereto—was trouble! His mind was already busy with the possibilities. A raid by sea from Karsten? He was certain no party from the duchy could have won through the mountains, not when all that country was patrolled by the Falconers of the heights and his own Borderer companies. Or was it some slash-and-go attempt on the part of Alizon, operating by sea? Their sullen unrest had been apparent for months. Or—

Simon's hands did not slack speed in pulling on boots or fastening belt, though his breath came a little faster as he thought on the third and worst possibility—the chance that Kolder was not crushed, that the evil—alien to this world in the same way he was alien—stirred again, moved, lapped closer to them.

In the months since that ruthless enemy had struck and been repulsed, since the Kolder stronghold on the island of Gorm had been taken and cleansed and their supported rising in Karsten failed, they had gone. Nothing stirred from their dark hold of Yle, though none of the Estcarp forces could break through the barrier which locked that cluster of towers from approach by sea or land. Simon, for one, did not believe that the defeat in Gorm had finished the Kolder threat. That would not be done with until the aliens were traced to their overseas stronghold and the nest there destroyed with the vipers in it. Such a move could not be made as yet—not while Karsten smoldered to the south or Alizon remained a battle hound hardly in check in the north.

He was listening now, not only with the sense he could not have named which had warned him out of sleep, but with his ears for the warning tocsin on the tower above. The Borderers who manned this keep were not to be taken unawares. Surely by now the alarm should be booming, vibrating through the stone of the walls!

"Simon!" The summons was so sharp and imperative that he swung around, weapon once again in his hand.

Jaelithe's face was pallid in this half-light, but her lips were unnaturally tight against her teeth. It might have been fear which lighted her eyes so—or was it? A soft crimson robe was clutched about her, held negligently by one hand. She had not put her arms into its wide sleeves and it dragged along the floor as she came around the end of the bed to him, walking stiffly as if in her sleep. But she was awake, very much awake, and that was not fear moving her.

"Simon—I—I am whole!"

It hit him, worse than the summons, with a hurt which registered deep, and which would grow and hurt the more; he sensed this fleetingly. So—it had meant that much to her? That she felt herself maimed, lessened by what had been between them. And another part of Simon, less troubled by emotion, arose to defend her. Witchdom had been her life. As all her sisterhood she had had pride of accomplishment, joy in that usage; yet she had willingly set aside, so she thought, all that when she had come to him, believing that in their uniting of bodies she would lose all which meant so much to her. And his second thought was so much the better one!

Simon held out his hand, though he longed to take her wholly into his arms. And her new joy which blazed from every part of her, as if a fire were lit deep within her skin, bones, and flesh, warmed him also as their clasp went tight, fingers locking about fingers.

"How—?" he began, but she interrupted him.

"It is with me still—it is! Oh, Simon, I am not only woman, but also witch!"

Her other hand dropped its hold on her robe so that the folds collapsed on the floor about her feet. Her fingers went to her breast, seeking what she no longer wore—the witch jewel she had surrendered at her wedding.

A little of that bright look faded as she realized she no longer possessed that tool through which the energy which filled her now could work. Then, with her old-time quick reaction to fact, she broke clasp with Simon and stood, her head slightly atilt, as if she too, listened.

"The alarm has not sounded." Simon stooped to gather up the robe and wrap her in it.

Jaelithe nodded. "I do not think this is an attack. But there is trouble—evil—on the move."

"Yes, but where—and what?"

She still stood in the attitude of one listening, but this time Simon knew that she did not hear audibly, but sensed some wave reaching directly to her mind. He felt it, too, that uneasiness which was fast heightening into a push to action. But what kind of action, where, against who, or what?

"Loyse!" A whisper. Jaelithe whirled and made for the coffer which held her clothing. She was dressing with the same haste as Simon had. But not in the robes of her household faring. What she burrowed deep to find was the soft leather which went under chain mail, the clothing of one riding on a foray.

Loyse? Simon could not be so sure, but he accepted her word without question. There were four of them, oddly assorted—four fighters for the freedom of Estcarp, for their own freedom from the evil which Kolder had sown so far in what had once been a fair world. Simon Tregarth, the alien from another world; Jaelithe, the Witch of Estcarp; Koris, exiled from Gorm before its fall into darkness, Captain of the Guard and then Seneschal and Marshal of Estcarp; and Loyse, the Heiress of Verlaine, a castle of wrecker lords on the coast. Fleeing a marriage with Yvian of Karsten, she had brought Jaelithe out of Verlaine, and together they had wrought subtly in Kars for the undoing of Yvian and all that he stood for. Loyse, wearing hauber, carrying sword and shield, had joined in the attack on Gorm. And in the citadel of Sippar had pledged herself to Koris. Loyse, the pale, small girl who was indeed a warrior strong and brave beyond most counting. And this sending dealt with danger for Loyse!

"But she is at Es Castle—" Simon protested, as he pulled on mail to match that which now clinked softly in Jaelithe's hands. And Es Castle was the heart, if the enemy had dared to strike there—!

"No!" Again Jaelithe was positive. "There is the sea—in this there is the sea."

"Koris?"

"I do not feel him, not in this. If I only had the jewel!" She was tugging on riding boots. "It is as if I tried to track a drifting mist. I can see the drift, but nothing is clear. But Loyse is in danger and the sea is part of it."

"Kolder?" Simon put into words' his deepest fear.

"No. There is not the blankness of the Kolder wall. But the need for help is great! We must ride, Simon—west and south." She had turned a little, her eyes now focused on the wall as if she could really see through it to the point she sought.

"We ride." He agreed.

The living quarters of the keep were yet silent. But as they sped together down the hallway to the stair they heard the sounds of the changing guard. Simon called, "Turn out the Riders!"

His words echoed hollowly, but carried, to be answered by a startled exclamation from below. Before he and Jaelithe were halfway down the stairs, Simon heard the piping of the alert.

This garrison was well prepared for sudden sallies.

10

Through spring and summer the alarm had sounded again and again to set the Borderers loose along the marches. Those who made up the striking force Simon commanded were largely recruited from the fugitive Old Race. Driven out of Karsten when the massacre orders of Kolder were given, they had many causes to hate the despoilers and murderers who now hold their lands and who came, in quick stab raids, to try the defenses of Estcarp, the last home of that dark-haired, dark-eyed race who carried ancient wisdom and strange blood, whose women had witch power and whose men were dour, stinging wasps of fighters.

"No beacon, Lord—"

Ingvald, Simon's second in command from the old days when they had fought, rode and fought again in the high hills, waited him in the courtyard. It was Jaelithe who answered.

"A sending, Captain."

The Karstenian refugee's eyes widened as he looked at her. But he did not protest.

"An attack here?"

"No. Trouble west and south." Simon made answer. "We ride fast—with half a troop. You remain in command here."

Ingvald hesitated as if he wished to argue that, but he did not speak except to say, "Durstan's company has the hill duty for this day and are ready to ride."

"Good enough."

One of the serving women ran from the hall behind them, holding a platter covered with rounds of journey bread, new from the oven and each bearing a smoking slice of meat. Behind her pounded a kitchen lad with filled beakers slopping their contents over his hands as he came. Jaelithe and Simon ate as they stood, watching the troop check mounts and supply bags, ready weapons, for the move out.

"The sender!" Simon heard a small, pleased laugh from Jaelithe.

"She knows! Had I but my jewel in again, we could dismiss her to other duties."

Simon blinked. So Jaelithe, even without her jewel, had communicated with the young witch who was their link with Estcarp command. The warning must even now be on its way to the Guardians' Council. In turn Jaelithe might be able to hold that communication as they rode, stretching it to report.

He began to consider the terrain west and south—mountains, the broken foothill country, and sea coast to the west. There were one or two small villages, market centers, but no other keep or castle. There were also temporary guard points, but all were too small, too far within Estcarp's own territory to house sending witches. So hill beacons passed warning. And there had been no such beacon lighted.

What was Loyse doing there? Why had she come forth from Es Castle and ridden into that wilderness?

"Brought by trick." Jaelithe was reading his surface thoughts again. "Though the manner of the tricking I cannot tell you. The purpose I think I can guess—"

"Yvian's move!" It was the most logical answer to any action against the heiress of Verlaine. By the laws of Karsten she was Yvian's wife, through whom he could claim Verlaine—though he had never set eyes on Loyse, nor she on him. Get her under his hand and the bargain Fulk had made for his daughter would be completed. Karsten was in uproar by all reports. Yvian, the mercenary who had won to power by might of arms, was facing the bared teeth of the old nobility. He would have to answer their hostility firmly or his ducal throne would crumble under him.

And Loyse was of the old blood; she could claim kins-rights with at least three of the most powerful houses. Using her as a tool Yvian's own ability could accomplish much. He had to put Karsten in order in a hurry. Though Simon knew that Estcarp had no intention of carrying war beyond her own borders—save in the direction of the Kolder—Yvian would not believe that.

The Duke of Karsten must rest very uneasy, knowing that his massacre of the Old Race gave more than a little reason to center the vengeance of the witches upon him. And he would not believe that they did not intend to attack him. Yes, Loyse was a weapon and a tool Yvian must be wild to get within his two hands for use.

They rode out of the keep at a purposeful trot, Jaelithe matching Simon's pace in the lead, Durstan's twenty men providing a competent fighting tail. The main road ran to the coast, perhaps four hours ride away. Before the fall of Sulcarkeep, the traders' city under Kolder attack, this had been one of the trade arteries of Estcarp, linking half a dozen villages and one fair-sized town with that free port of the merchant-rovers. Since Sulcarkeep had been blasted into rubble nearly a year ago the last despairing gesture of its garrison, taking with it most of its enemy, the highway had lost most of its traffic and the signs of its disuse were visible, save where the patrols worked to keep it free of fallen trees and storm wrack.

The troop clattered through Romsgarth, a central gathering point for the farms of the slopes. Since it was not market day their swift passage awoke interest from the early stirring townsfolk and there were calls of inquiry as they passed. Simon saw Durstan wave to the town guard, and knew they would leave a watchful and ready post behind them. The Old Race might be destined to go down to defeat, their neighbors snarling at their borders. But they would take a large number of those enemies with them in the final battle. And that knowledge was one of the things which kept Alizon and Karsten from yet making the fatal move of outright invasion.

Some leagues beyond Romsgarth Jaelithe signaled a halt. She rode barehead, her helmet swinging at her saddle horn. And now she turned her head slowly from right to left, as if she could scent the path of the quarry. But Simon had already caught the trace.

"There!" The sensation of danger which had been with him since waking focused unerringly. A track split south from the main road. Across it lay a fallen tree and that trunk bore fresh scars on its bark. One of the troop dismounted to inspect.

"Scrapes of hooves—recent—"

"Infiltrate," Simon ordered.

They spread out, not to use the artery of the half-closed path, but working in through brush, among trees. Jaelithe took up her helmet.

"Make haste!"

This ground was right for ambush; to run into attack was the choice of a fool. But Simon nodded. What had brought them here was building to a climax. Jaelithe pressed heels to her mount, jumped the log, headed down the path with Simon spurring to catch up with her again. To any watcher it might seem they were alone, his men remained behind.

The wind in their faces was sea-scented. Somewhere ahead an inlet in the coast waited. Was a ship there—to make a quick pickup and then to sea—to Karsten? What *had* brought Loyse into such danger? He wished for the Falconers and their trained birds to spy on what lay ahead.

Simon could hear the rustling advance of his men— they would certainly not go unheralded in this country. His mount flung up its head and neighed—to be answered from ahead. Then they came out in an open pocket of meadow sloping gently to beach in a cove. Two horses grazed there, saddles empty. And well out stood a ship, its painted sail belly-rounded by the wind, it was far beyond their reaching.

Jaelithe dismounted, ran towards a splotch of color on the beach and Simon followed her. He stood looking down at a woman. Her face was oddly blank and calm, though both her hands were tight upon the blade which

had been driven into her. To Simon she was a stranger.
"Who?"

Jaelithe frowned. "I have seen her. She was from
across the mountains. Her name—" From storehouse of
memory she produced it in triumph. "Her name was
Berthora and she once lived in Kars!"

"Lord!"

Simon looked to where one of the troop beckoned.
He went to see what was mounted on the very edge of
the wave-lapped shore. A spear driven deep into the
sand so that it stood uprightly defiant held a mail gauntlet. He did not need any words of explanation. Karsten
had been and gone, and wanted that coming and going
known. Yvian had declared open battle. Simon's hand
closed upon that gauge and pulled it loose.

2   BORDER FORAY

THE RAYS of the lights centered on the glittering thing
in the middle of the board, making it seem to ripple
with a mindless life of its own. Yet it was but a glove,
sweat-stained leather palm down, mailed back up.

"She left two days ago, but the why no one can say—"
Bleak voice from which the fellowship had chilled away,
leaving only grim purpose. Koris of Gorm stood at the
end of the table, leaning forward, his hands so tight
about the haft of his war ax that his knuckles were
sharp ridges. "Last eve—last *eve* I discovered it! By
what devil's string was she tolled here?"

"We can take it," Simon replied, "that this is Karsten's

doing and the why we can guess." More "whys" than one, he thought, and meeting Jaelithe's gaze, knew that she shared that guess or guesses. With Koris so emotionally involved this kidnaping would upset the delicate balance of Estcarp defense. Not even witch power was going to keep the young seneschal from Loyse's trail, at least not until he had a chance to cool off and begin to really think again. But had that ship borne away Jaelithe would he, Simon, have been any the different?

"Kars falls." A simple statement, fact when delivered in that tone of voice.

"Just like that?" Simon retorted. For Koris to go whirling over the border now with such a force as he could gather in a hurry was the worst stupidity Simon knew. "Yes, Kars falls—but by planning, not by attack without thought behind it."

"Koris—" Jaelithe's long-fingered hand came out into the light which had gathered about Yvian's battle gage, "do not lessen Loyse!"

She had his attention, had broken through to him when Simon had failed.

"Lessen her?"

"Remember Briant. Do not separate those in your mind now, Koris."

Briant and Loyse—again she was right, his witch-wife; Simon gave respect where it was due. Loyse had ridden as the blank-shield mercenary Briant, had lived with Jaelithe in Kars, keeping watch in the very maw of the enemy, just as she had stormed into Sippar. And as Briant she had not only won free of Verlaine, but brought the captive Jaelithe with her at the beginning of her adventure, when all the might of that castle and its lord had been arrayed against her. The Loyse who was also Briant was no helpless maiden, but had a mind, will, and skills of her own.

"She is Yvian's—by their twisted laws!" Koris' ax moved into the light in a sweeping arc which bit deep, severing the stuff of the gauntlet as if it had been fashioned of clay.

"No—she is her own until she wills it otherwise, Koris. What manner of mischief was wrought to get her into their hands, I do not understand. But that it can hold her I doubt. However, think on this, my proud captain. Go you slashing into Kars as you wish, and she will then be a weapon for Yvian. The Kolder taint still lies there—and would you have her used against you as they can do?"

Koris' head turned to her, he looked up to meet her gaze as he must always do from his dwarfish height. His too-wide shoulders were a little hunched, so that he had almost the stance of an animal poised for a killing leap.

"I do not leave her there." Again a statement of fact.

"Nor do we," Simon agreed. "But look you—they will expect us to be after such bait, and the trap will be waiting."

Koris blinked. "So—and what then do you urge? To leave her wrest herself free? She had great courage—my lady—but she is not a witch. Nor can she, one against many, fight a war on her own!"

Simon was ready. Luckily he had had those few hours, before Koris and his guard had come pelting into the keep, to do some planning. Now he slapped a parchment map down beside the ax head still dividing the severed gauntlet.

"We do not ride directly for Kars. We could not reach that city without a full army and then we needs must fight all the way. Our van will enter the city at Yvian's invitation."

"Behind a war horn?" Koris demanded. "Shape changing—?" He was not so hostile now, beginning to think.

"After a fashion," Simon told him. "We move here . . ."

There was a risk. He had been considering such an operation for weeks, but heretofore he had thought the balance against it too great. Now that they needed a lever against Karsten it was the best he could think of.

Koris studied the map. "Verlaine!" From that dot he glanced at Simon.

"Yvian wants Verlaine, has wanted it from the start. That was partly his reason for wedding Loyse. Not only does the wreckers' treasure stored there beckon him—remember his men are mercenaries and must be paid when there is no loot in prospect—but that castle can also give him a raiders' port from which to operate against us. And now, with the loot from the Old Race exhausted, he will need Verlaine the more. Fulk has been very wise, not venturing to Yvian's territory. But suppose he would—"

"Trade Verlaine for Loyse! You mean that is what we shall do?" Koris' handsome face was frown twisted.

"Allow Yvian to believe he is going to get Verlaine without any trouble." Simon put together the ideas he had been holding in mind. As he spoke Koris' frown faded, he had concentration of a general picking at a piece of strategy seeking weaknesses. But he did not interrupt as Simon continued adding the facts which his scouts had garnered to the reports of the Falconers, lacing the whole together with his knowledge of such warfare from the past.

"A ship on the rocks will bring them out to plunder. Fulk will have a guard still in the castle, yes. But they will not be watching the ways within his own walls which he does not know. Those were Loyse's ways and my lady knows them. A party coming down from the mountains will burrow in thus, and the heart of the keep is ours. We can settle then with those combing the shore for loot."

"It will take time—and a storm—at the proper day and luck—" But Koris' protests were feather-light and Simon knew it. The seneschal would agree to his plan; the danger of a head-long storming into enemy territory was past. At least as long as Koris could be occupied with Verlaine.

"As for time," Simon rolled up the map, "we have

been moving to this goal for a day or more. I have sent a message to the Falconers and they have infiltrated the peaks. There are Borderer scouts who know every trail in that cutback, and Sulcarmen will man one of the derelicts from Sippar harbor. With new sails it will ride well enough, the water-logging setting it deep enough in the waves to seem full cargoed, and it can bear merchant symbols of Alizon. The storm—"

Jaelithe laughed. "Ah, the storm! Do you forget that wind and wave are liegemen to us, Simon? I shall see to wind and wave when the hour ripens."

"But—?" Koris looked up at her again in open question.

"But you deem me now powerless, Koris? It is far otherwise, I assure you!" Her voice rang out joyfully. "Let me but claim back my jewel and you shall have the proof of that. So, Simon, while you ride for the border and your spider's web about Fulk's hold, I will speed to Es Castle and that which I must have again."

He nodded. But deep within him that faint pain pricked once again. She had laid aside the jewel for him —seemingly with joy and content. Only now that she knew she was not bereft of what she thought she had lost, that sacrifice no sacrifice at all, she had put on once again that old cloak to cover the inner places she had revealed to him. And between them was the shadow of division. A chill grew from his fear. Would that division grow stronger—perhaps into a wall? Simon thrust the thoughts away; there was Verlaine to consider now.

Simon sent out the summoning—not by hill beacon which would alert any Karstenian spy in the heights— but by witch sending where it was possible, by rider where it was not. The hill garrisons were thinned—here five men, there ten or a dozen. And those so chosen rode in small parties into the mountains as if on routine patrol, to keep apart until the final word.

Koris dealt with Anner Osberic whose Sulcar merchant-raiders had homed to Es Port now that their coast keep was lost. There was a move to take over Gorm as a base. But as yet men shunned that tragic isle in the bay with its haunted city of Sippar, where the citadel left by the Kolder was sealed under the will of the Guardians of Estcarp, lest the outland knowledge of the enemy be ill-used. Osberic's father had died at Sulcar-keep, his hate for the Kolder and all their ilk ran sea-deep and harsh as any storm, and his knowledge of wind and wave, while not that of a witch, was great. If he could not control storms, he could ride them. And he and his men had been demanding action against the enemy. This dangerous game with a wreckers' castle for the bait would please them greatly.

The plan was in motion, all they needed was an agreed striking time. Simon lay flat on a crag ledge. The day was gray, but no fog spoiled his watch of the rounded walls, the two sky-arching towers which were Verlaine. He cupped in his hand one of Estcarp's equivalents of field glasses, a lens of transparent quartz. Down in that gazing oval was tiny, but very distinct and clear, one of the claw-shaped reefs which harvested the sea for the wreckers. Anner would put his pseudo-merchantman on course to crack up on that reef, about mid-point—far enough from the castle to draw the men well away from the walls, but not so far as to suggest danger in garnering the wreckage.

The gray sky, the moist air, warned of a storm. But they needed a controlled fury to work on time schedule. Simon continued to check the terrain before him via glass, but his thoughts strayed. Jaelithe had gone to Es Castle and the Guardians, alive and vibrant in her exultation over her discovery that as a witch she had not been rendered impotent. But since then, no word from out of the north that bore any news of her, none of that mental touch Simon had come to expect as a tie between them. Almost he could believe now that those weeks in South Keep had been a dream, that he had never held the fulfillment of desires he had never realized existed within him, until they had become wrapped in flesh and blood in his arms; he now knew a place which was beyond earth and stars, beyond self, when another shared it.

And that chill fear which had been only a spark in the beginning grew, that wall he sensed took on solid shape. So that he must strive to keep his thoughts away from that path lest he, too, as Koris might, go storming away from duty to seek her.

Time was short, very short. This night, Simon thought, as he slipped the seeing stone back in his belt pocket, this night ought to see their move. Before she had left him Jaelithe had laid the knowledge of the underground ways into his mind. Last night he, Ingvald and Durstan had descended into the cave which was the beginning of those passages, gazed unwillingly at the ancient altar there, raised to gods long since vanished with the dust of those who had worshiped them. They had felt also that throat-choking residue of *something* which still hung there, which fed upon Simon's own gift of extra-sense, until he had to impose iron control on his shaking body. More than one sort of power had been in use on this somber continent of an old, old world.

He slipped down from the crag now, made his way to the pocket where three of the Borderer scouts and a Falconer sat cross-legged, as if they would warm themselves at a fire they dared not light.

"No word?"

A foolish question, Simon thought, even as he asked it. He would have known it if she were here. But the boy in the leather and mail of the scout force came lithely to his feet to answer.

"Message from the seneschal, Lord. Captain Osberic has the ship readied. He will loose her on signal, but does not know how long the wind will serve."

Time . . . Simon tried to gauge the wind, though he did not have any sea knowledge. If Jaelithe did not come—then still they must move and risk the greater peril inherent in a true storm, with no aid of witch-craft. It must be tonight, or no later than tomorrow.

A sharp bird call and the black-and-white falcon that was ears and eyes for Uncar spiraled down to settle on its master's fist.

"The seneschal comes," Uncar reported.

Simon had never understood the tie between man and bird, but he had long ago learned that such reports were accurate and that the hawk range of the Falconers was far more effective than any human scouting in these heights. Koris was on the prowl, and this time Simon would have to agree with the other's urging to move. But where was Jaelithe?

In spite of his ungainly body Koris moved with the economy of action marking an experienced fighting man. The huge ax he had taken from the hand of legendary Volt in the bird-god's hidden tomb was muffled in a riding cloak, but he wore his winged helmet and came armed for battle. That handsome face, so ill supported by his misshapen body, was grimly alight as Simon had seen it before upon occasion.

"This night we move! Anner says that wind and wave favor us. He can not promise so later." He hesitated and then added in a lower voice, "There is no word from the north."

"So be it! Pass the signal, Waldis. At dusk we move."

The boy disappeared arrow-swift between the rocks. Uncar's lean face showed within the narrow opening of his bird-head helm.

"The rain comes. It will favor us that much more. At dusk, March Warder—" Hawk on wrist he followed Waldis, to bring up his men.

There was no true sunset; the gathering clouds were far too heavy. And the wave action was stronger. Soon Osberic would loose his bait ship. The wreckers had three watch points—two on the reef and one on the center tower of the hold; all would be manned in ill weather. Those on the reef need not be feared, but the sentry post on the tower also overlooked those fields through which the attackers must move. And though they had marked every bit of cover on that approach, Simon was worried. An early rain would give them cover.

But the storm winds came before the rain. And they had only the dusk to cloak them as the line of Borderers and Falconers sifted down to the entrance hole, climbed into the dark beneath. There was a sudden gleam and Simon heard an exclamation from Koris.

The blade of Volt's ax shone with light. And Simon sensed a stir of the force from the crumbling altar, the rising of an energy beyond his ability to describe, but one he feared.

"A battle light!" Koris' humorless laugh followed. "I thank you, Volt, for this added favor!"

"Move!" Simon ordered. "You do not know what may wake here with that blade!"

They found the entrance to the passage quickly. There was a tingling in Simon's skin, his hair lifting despite the weight of his helmet, answering the electricty in this place. Here the walls were slimed with oily streaks of moisture which shown in their journey lights, and a moldering, rotten stench thickened as they went. Underfoot, the flooring vibrated to the pound of rising waves not too far away.

A stair before them, where silvery trails crossed and recrossed the stone, as if giant slugs had made highways there for countless generations. Up and up, all Jaelithe's knowledge of these passages was gained during her flight through them. Loyse had discovered and used them for her purposes, and Simon wished he had her direction now. But he must be certain of his goal and not explore. They would emerge in the tower chamber which had once been Loyse's; from there they could spread to take Fulk's hold—always providing the bulk of his garrison were occupied elsewhere.

The steps rose endlessly, and then Simon's counting ceased. There were still steps ahead, but this landing had counted out correctly for the door. And he could see the simple latch which held on this side. Luckily, the builder who had devised these ways had not concealed such catches. He bore down and a five-foot oval swung away.

Even here they had to use journey lights for the room was dark. A canopied cavern of a bed faced them. There was a chest at its foot, another under the window slits outside of which howled storm wind.

"Signal!" Simon need not have given that order. One of Koris' guard had leaped on the chest, his arm up to thrust open the covering on the slit. Then the beat of the vibration pattern winked through all their journey lights, as it would through Anner Osberic's if he were in position. The ship would be released. Now they had only to wait until the alarm of her coming would awake the castle.

But that waiting was the worst for all of them, keyed to action as they were. Two small parties, one under Ingvald, and one of Falconers under Uncar's command, went back to the wall ways to explore. Uncar reported another door giving upon an empty sleeping chamber, providing a second exit.

Still time dragged and Simon mentally listed the many things which might go wrong. Fulk would be prepared for invasion from without. He had his scouts, as they had discovered in the pass. But this passage had never been discovered as far as Loyse knew.

"Ahhhh—" Someone nearby breathed a sigh of relief, which was swallowed in a blast of brazen clamor from just above their heads, startling them all.

"That is it!" Koris caught at Simon's shoulder and then pushed past him to the door of the chamber. "The wreck tocsin! That will shake these rats out of their holes!"

3 BLACK NIGHT

PATIENCE. Long ago Loyse had learned patience. Now she must use it again as a weapon against fear and the panic which was chill in her, a choking band about her throat, a crushing weight upon her. Patience—and her wits—that was all they had left her.

It was quiet enough in this room where she had been left to herself at long last. There was no need to rise from the chair and try the window shutters or the door. They had even stripped the bed curtains from their supports. Lest she try some mischief against herself, she supposed. But it had not come to that yet; oh, no, not to that. Loyse's lips shaped a shadow smile, but the glint in her eyes was not that of amusement.

She felt very faint, and it was hard to think clearly when the room spun in dizzy side-slips from time to time. Nausea had racked her on board the coasting ship—then she had not eaten for a long time.

How long a time? She began to reckon childishly on her fingers, turning them down in turn, trying to put a memory to each. Three, four, five days?

A face etched on her mind for all time—the dark-haired woman who had come to her in Es Castle in the early morning with a tale. What tale?

Loyse fought for a clear memory of that meeting. And the fear cloud grew thicker as she realized that this was no mental haziness born of nausea and shock, this was a blocking out which had no connection with *her* body or emotions. There had been a woman—Berthora! Loyse had a flash of triumph when she was able

25

to set name to the woman. And Berthora had brought her out of Es Castle with a message.

But what was that message and from whom? Why, oh, why had she been so secretive about riding forth from Es with Berthora? There were fleeting memories of a wood road, and a storm—with the two of them sheltering among rocks while rain and wind made fury in the night. Then, a meadow sloping to the sea where they waited.

Why? Why had she remained there so calmly with Berthora, feeling no uneasiness, no warning! Ensorcelled? Had she been power-moved? But no—that she could not believe. Estcarp was friend, not enemy. And now that Loyse pieced together these ragged tatters of memory, she was very certain that Berthora had moved in haste and as a fugitive in enemy territory. Did Karsten also have its witches?

Loyse pressed her hands against her cheeks, cold flesh meeting cold flesh. To believe that was to negate all she knew of her own land. There were no witches in Karsten since the Old Race had been three times horned, outlawed to be killed on sight. Yet she was certain, just as certain, that she had been spellbound, spell-led, to that meeting with the ship from the south.

There was something more—something about Berthora. She must remember, for it was important! Loyse bit her knuckles and fought her queasiness, the haze in her mind, fought grimly to remember. At last she achieved a bit of a picture . . .

Berthora crying out—first in entreaty, and then in despairing anger—though it was her tone rather than her words that Loyse recalled. And one of those from the ship striking at her with a callous casualness. Berthora stumbling back, her hands on the sword which had given her death, so fast upon that blade that its owner could not pull it free. Then an order, and another man bending over Berthora, fumbling in her riding tunic, bringing forth a hand clenched about something, something Loyse had not seen.

Berthora had delivered her to Karsten, and had been paid with death. But to aid in that delivering Berthora had had some weapon beyond Loyse's knowledge.

How it had been done must not concern her now. That it was done . . . Loyse forced her hand down from her mouth, made it rest on her knee. She was in Kars, in Yvain's hold. If they had sought her in Estcarp, were seeking her now, they could only conjure as to where she had been taken. As for plucking her forth again— It would take an army to break open Karsten, such an army as Estcarp could not put in the field. Loyse had listened enough to the councils of war to know just how precarious was the Old Kingdom. Let them strip the country to invade Karsten and Alizon would snap down from the north.

In Verlaine once she had been one against all the might of Fulk, with no friend within that sea-pounded pile. Here she was one against many again. If she did not feel so sick and dizzy she could think more clearly! But to move made the floor under her dusty riding boots heave and roll as had the deck of the coaster.

The door opened and a flare of a hand lamp struck at her through the dusk, blinding her so that she must squint up at those who stood there. Three of them, two in the livery of ducal servants, one holding the lamp, the other a tray of covered dishes. But the third, that slender figure with a scarf about head and shoulders in masking concealment—

Putting down lamp and tray on the table the serving women left, closing the door behind them. Only when they had gone did that other come into the full light, twitch aside her veiling to view Loyse eye to eye.

She stood taller than the heiress of Verlaine, and her figure had a delicate grace Loyse could not claim. She wore her fair hair looped in intricate plaiting, the whole snooded in a gem-spangled net. And there were more jewels at her throat, her girdle, braceleting her arms above the tight fabric of her sleeves, ringing each finger. As if she had set out the wealth of her gem caskets with purpose to overawe the beholder. Yet, looking beyond all that glitter to her calm eyes, her serene expression, Loyse thought such a gesture could only be a screen. The wearer of that wealth might do it because it was expected of her, not because she needed support of her treasures at this meeting.

Now her hand, with its glinting burden, advanced and she picked up the lamp to hold it higher, facing Loyse with a measuring look which stung, but under which the girl sat unmoving. She could not match the other's beauty. Where this one was golden-haired, Loyse was bleached to fading; where this one was all grace, not studied but instinctive, Loyse was awkward angularity. Nor could she pride herself as to wit, for the Lady Aldis was noted for her astute moves in the murky waters of Yvian's court.

"You must have more to you than appears," Aldis broke the silence first. "But that lies far buried, my lady duchess." The sober appraisal of that speech became mockery at its close.

Lamp still in hand, Aldis swept a curtsy which made her skirts swing in a graceful swirl not one woman in a hundred could have equaled. "My lady duchess, you are served—pray partake. Doubtless the fare upon which you were forced to break your fast of late has not been of the best."

She returned the lamp to the table and drew up a stool, her manners a subtly contemptuous counterfeit of a servant's deference. When Loyse neither moved nor answered, Aldis set forefinger to lip as if puzzled, and then smiled.

"Ah—I have not been named to your fair grace, have I? My name is Aldis, and it is my pleasure to welcome you to this, your city of Kars where you have long been awaited. Now, does it please you to dine, my lady duchess?"

"Is it not rather your city of Kars?" Loyse put no inflection into that question, it was as simply asked as a child might do. She knew not what role might aid her now, but to have Yvian's mistress underrate his unwilling wife seemed a good move.

Aldis' smile grew brighter. "Ill-natured tittle-tattle, gossip, such as should never have reached your ears, my lady duchess. When the chatelaine is missing, then there needs must be someone to see that all is done mannerly, as our lord duke would wish. I flatter myself in believing that you shall find little here, your fair grace, that must be changed."

A threat—a warning? Yet if either, most lightly delivered in a tone which gave no emphasis. But Loyse believed that Aldis had no intention of yielding what power she had here to a wife married for reasons of state.

"The report of your death was a sad blow to our lord duke," Aldis continued. "Where he was prepared to welcome a bride, came instead an account of an open tower window, a piece of torn robe, and the sea beneath—as if those waves were more welcome than his arms! A most upsetting thought to haunt our lord duke's pillow by night. And how greatly relieved he was when came that other report—that Loyse of Verlaine had been bewitched out of her senses by those hags of the north, taken by them as hostage. But now all is well again, is it not? You are in Kars with a hundred hundred swords to keep a safe wall between you and the enemy. So eat, my lady duchess, and then rest. The hour is not far off when you must look your best to ravish the eyes of your bridegroom." The mockery was no longer light—cat-claws unsheathed to tear the deeper.

Aldis lifted the covers from the dishes on the tray and the odor of the food turned Loyse's emptiness into a sudden pain. This was no time for pride or defiance.

She smeared her hand across her eyes as might a child who is come to the end of a crying bout, and got to her feet, clutching at the bed post to steady her steps. A lurch brought her to the table edge and she worked her way along the board to drop onto the stool.

"Poor child! You are indeed foredone—" But Aldis made no move to approach her and for that Loyse was thankful. A small part of her resented fiercely that the other watched while she had to use both hands to bring a goblet to her lips; her weakness was a betrayal.

But Aldis did not matter now. What did was restoring the wavering strength of her body, clearing her head. That Aldis had come here might in turn lead to something. Though Loyse could not yet see the advantage in the visit.

Warmth from the liquid she swallowed spread through her; the surface fear ebbed. Loyse put down the goblet. She did not want a wine-born muzziness clouding her thoughts. Now she pulled a bowl of soup to her and began to spoon it up, the savor of it reaching her. Duke Yvian was well served by his cooks. Against her will Loyse relaxed, relished her supper.

"Boar in red wine," Aldis commented brightly. "A dish you shall find often before you, lady, since our gracious lord relishes it. Jappon, the chief cook, has a master hand for it. My lord duke expects us to mark his likes and dislikes and be attentive to them."

Loyse took another sip of wine. "Vintage of a good year," she commented, striving to hold her voice to the same even lightness. "It would seem that this lord duke of yours has also a palate. I would have believed tavern wine more to his taste, since his first man draughts came from such casks—"

Aldis smiled more sweetly. "Our lord duke does not mind allusions to his somewhat—shall we say—irregular beginnings. That he won Karsten by the might of his sword arm—"

"*And* the backing of his blank-shields," Loyse cut in blandly.

"And the loyalty of his followers," Aldis agreed. "He feels pride in that fact and often speaks of it in company."

"One who climbs to heights must beware of the footing," Loyse broke a slice of the nut-flour bread in twain and nibbled its crust.

"One who rises to heights makes very sure that the footing on that height is smoothed," Aldis countered. "He has learned not to leave aught to chance, for Fortune is fickle."

"And wisdom must balance all swords," Loyse replied with a hill proverb. The food had drawn her out of her misery. But—no over-confidence. Yvian was no stupid sword swinger, easily befooled. He *had* won Karsten by wits as well as fighting. And this Aldis— Walk softly, Loyse, walk softly, beware of every leaf rustle.

"Our lord duke is paramount in all things, with sword, in the council chamber and—in bed. Nor is his body misshapen—"

Loyse hoped her sudden freeze had gone unnoted, but she doubted that. And Aldis' next oblique shaft confirmed that doubt.

"They speak of great deeds done in the north, and that a certain misborn, misshapen churl who swings a stolen ax there led the van—"

"So?" Loyse yawned and then yawned again. Her fatigue was not pretended. "Rumor always wags a wide tongue. I have eaten; is it now permitted that I sleep?"

"But, my lady duchess, you speak as one who considers herself a prisoner. Whereas you are paramount lady in all Kars and Karsten!"

"A thing I shall keep in mind. But still, that thought, as uplifting as it is, gives me not as much joy as some rest would do. I bid you good eve, my Lady Aldis."

Another smile, a tinkle of laughter, and she did go. But nothing covered the sound Loyse listened for—the scrape of key in lock. Paramount lady she might be in Kars, but this night she was also prisoner within this chamber—and the key lay in other hands. Loyse sucked her lower lip against her teeth as she considered what that might lead to.

She gave the room a measuring survey. The uncurtained bed, as was usual in a room of state, stood on a two step dais above the flooring. There were windows in two walls. But as she loosed the inner shutters of one after another, she discovered beyond a netting of metal mesh through which she might thrust her fingers to the second joint, but no farther to freedom.

There was a chest against the far wall, wherein lay some garments she did not examine past the first glance. But she was still tired, her whole body ached to stretch out on the bed. There was one more task she set herself to, and it was one which left her weak and trembling. Sleep she must, but no one would come upon her unawares, for the table was now an inner barrier across the door.

Though she was so tired she felt that it would require a vast effort to raise her hand to her head, sleep did not come as Loyse lay there, staring up into the rafter frame which had supported canopy and curtains. She had not turned down the lamp and that made a fine glow by which she could see every part of the chamber.

In the past she had known a similar disquiet—strongest of all in that temple or shrine of the forgotten race where the hidden passages of Verlaine opened to the clean sky. The hidden ways of Verlaine . . . For a moment it was as if their dankness, the acrid odor of them, was about her now. Witchcraft! You could sniff it when you had known it before. Loyse's nostrils pinched as she drew in a deep lungful of air. After all, she did not know all the secrets of Estcarp—and once before she had had a part of one here in Kars, while she and Jaelithe had fished in many pools for such scraps of information as might aid the northern cause. So there could still be agents of the Guardians hereabouts.

The girl's hands balled into the covers on either side of her thin body. If she only had a measure of their power! If she could loose a sending now—to be picked up by a receptive, friendly mind! She willed that fiercely, crying soundlessly—not really for help, but for a steadying sense of companionship. She had been alone once, but then had come Jaelithe, and Simon, the tall stranger whom she had instinctively trusted and—and Koris. A faint flush warmed her cheeks as she remembered Aldis' sneers. Misborn, misshapen. Not true—never true! Mixed blood, yes—so that he united two strains to his own despite—the squat, powerful body of his Tor mother's kin, the handsome head of his noble Gorm father. But above all men the one her heart fixed upon from the day she had found him with Simon, wearing blank-shield disguises, outside the gate here in Kars, drawn by Jaelithe's sending.

Drawn by a sending . . . But she could not send! Once more Loyse fought her inner barrier, striving to break through. For there *was* the scent of witchcraft or at least of some other thing hereabouts. She was so sure of that! It roughened her skin, made her alert, waiting.

Loyse slipped from the bed, went to set her hands on the table across the doorway. Her arms straightened, she was pushing at that barrier. But something in her still unlulled, still awake, battled against that compulsion to do this.

She backed away to the foot of the bed, facing the door. The key clicked, the latch loosed. The heavy slab swung back. Aldis again! For a moment Loyse relaxed. Then she stared into the other's face. It was the same, exactly the same, feature by lovely feature. Yet—no!

And how it had changed she could not tell. There was even a little mocking smile still playing about those generously curved lips, the same expression on the fair face. Only Loyse knew, with every inch of her, that this was not the Aldis she had seen before.

"You are afraid," Aldis' voice, also. Exact—yet—no! "You have a right to fear, my lady duchess. Our lord duke does not like to be crossed. And you have played him several ill turns. He must make you truly his wife, you know that, or his purpose will not be served. And I do not think you will relish the manner of his wooing. No, I do not believe you shall find him a gentle lover willing to sue for your accord in the matter! Because you are in some ways a trouble to me, I shall allow you this much, my lady duchess."

Flashing through the air to land on the bed by her right hand—a dagger. More a lady's toy than the belt knives she had worn sheathed at her own hip, but still a weapon.

"A sting for you," the Aldis who was not Aldis continued, her voice falling to a soft murmur so that now Loyse could hardly understand her words. "I wonder how you will choose to use it, lady duchess, Loyse of Verlaine, in one way—or another?"

Then she was gone. Loyse stared at the heavy wood of the now closed door, wondering how she had vanished so swiftly. As if she had been a thing without corporal body—an illusion.

Illusion! The weapon and defense of a witch. Had Aldis indeed ever stood there? Or was this some move on the part of an Estcarpian agent who could only aid Yvian's captive in so much? But she would not nurse that thread of hope unduly.

Loyse turned to look at the bed, more than half expecting to find the blade gone, an illusion. But no. It lay there and under her hand it was solid, the whole slim length of it to needle point. The girl brought it to her breast, fondled it from simple cross hilt to that point. So she was to use it, was she? On whom? Yvian or herself? The choice had not seemed to matter to Aldis, or the semblance of Aldis, who had brought it to her.

4 *FULK AND—FULK!*

SIMON STOOD on the mid-step of the stair listening. Below was the din of battle where the forces of Estcarp mopped up the main hall. The loud "Sul! Sul!" of the Sulcarmen echoed faintly to him. But he strained to hear something else; movement above. He had not been mistaken, of that he was sure. Somewhere ahead on this narrow stair was Fulk. And the cornered lord of Verlaine had the advantage of anyone who dare follow him to his last stand.

There! Scrape of metal on stone? What sort of a surprise was Fulk preparing for his pursuers? Yet Fulk, above all, they must take in order to carry out their plan for Karsten. And time worked against them as Fulk's ally.

Simon edged on, his left shoulder pressed to the wall. So far their plan was working. The wrecked ship on the reef had opened Fulk's shore gates, sent out his men, centered the attention of the keep there. So that the invaders had nearly occupied the hold before the castle garrison was aware of their move.

But that had not led to quick surrender; rather the wreckers fought as men must who have no escape behind, and an unforgiving enemy before. Only because Simon had been sent spinning out of one swirling segment of the hall battle had he seen the flight of the tall man, his helm gone so that his red-gold mane identified him. Unlike Fulk of all the legends Simon had heard, this skulker did not seek to rally his men, take the lead in the next furious drive against the Borderers. Instead he had dodged, ran, sought this inner stair. And Simon, still with head ringing from the blow which had shaken him out of the press, followed.

Again, metal on stone. He was very sure of it. Some other weapon more, forceful than sword or ax being readied? The stair took an abrupt turn to the right just beyond, a yard-square landing was all he could see, the step up the other angle hidden. There was a globe light burning, but pallidly.

The light flickered. Simon drew a quick breath. If the lamp was on the verge of failing . . . But the flickering followed a pulsating pattern, almost as if its power had been sapped at regular intervals. Simon took another step, and another—the third would bring him to the landing and so exposed to what might be waiting on the other flight of stairs.

Flicker, flicker—he found himself counting those blinks. And now he was sure that each drained energy. Simon had never learned the secret of the globe lamps, they could be governed in intensity by tapping on wall plates set below each one. But as far as he knew the globes themselves never had to be renewed, and no one in Estcarp had been able to explain how they worked. Set in these castle piles ages ago their secret was forgotten.

Flicker again. Now the light was much dimmer. Simon whirled about the angle of the stair, his back to the wall, his dart gun ready. Four, six steps up and then the smooth forward run of a narrow corridor. At the top of those steps a barricade, stuff hastily dragged from rooms above. Was Fulk lying in wait to pick off the first to disturb that erection of stools and a table?

Somehow Simon was worried. Fulk's actions were so contrary to all he had heard of the coast-lord. These were the moves of a man trying to buy time. Time for what? All Fulk's forces were engaged below; he could not be attempting to assemble a relief. No, he was striving to get out himself! Why he was so certain of that Simon did not know, but he was convinced it was so.

Did Fulk know of an inner wall passage, was he hunting the exit now? No more sounds except that the muffled clamor from below lessened, the last of Fulk's men must be cut down.

The blink, blink of the light grew feebler. Then he did hear a faint sound, and fighter's instinct sent him scrambling down the stair angle. The white flash of an explosion! Simon, blinded by that glare, almost lost his footing. He rubbed his eyes.

Light, but no sound at all. Whatever force had been unleashed there was new to him. Now trails of smoke, acrid and throat rasping. Simon coughed, fought to see, but his eyes were still dazzled by the flash.

"Simon! What is here?"

Pound of feet on the stair. Simon caught a hazy glimpse of a winged helm.

"Fulk," he answered. "Up there—but watch—"

"Fulk!" Koris' long arm was out, solidly against the wall, supporting Simon. "But what does he up there?"

"What mischief he can, lord." More steps on the stair and Ingvald's voice to identify them.

"He is late to our meeting," Koris commented.

"Do not rush in—" At last he was able to see again. But the light globe was now far sped. Simon slipped up on the landing, forestalling Koris. The flimsy barrier was gone. Some charred bits of wood, a drift of ash and stains on the wall marked its site.

No sound, no movement from the hall or from the doors opening into that way. Step by step Simon advanced. Then he heard a small scuffling from behind the first door. Before he could move the great ax of Volt swung down to hit that barrier. The door gave and they looked into a room, the window facing them was open, a trail of rope hung out of it, anchored within by the weight of a chest.

Koris laid the ax on the floor and set his hands to the rope. All the strength of his great shoulders and arms went into an upward pull as Simon and Ingvald moved to the window.

The night was dark, but not too shadowed to hide the scene below. That rope, meant to drop Fulk to a lower roof, was now ascending, even with Fulk's weight upon it, past the point where the wrecker lord would dare leap free. Only—

Simon saw the white oval which was Fulk's face turned up to him. The dangling man, coming up to their waiting grasp through a series of pulls by Koris, deliberately loosened his hold on that line. He screamed aloud, a dreadful cry, as if he were protesting against his own action. Had he, until that last second, really believed he had a chance to land safely? But when he crashed down he lay there. An arm was lifted and fell again.

"He is still alive." Simon reached for the rope. He did not understand the need which moved him now, but he must look upon Fulk's face.

"I must go down," he added as the rope end whipped in the window and he sat about making it fast to his own waist.

"There is more in this than seems?" Koris asked.

"I believe so."

"Then down with you. But take care, even a broken-backed serpent wears fangs in its jaws. And Fulk has no reason to let his enemies live after him."

Simon scrambled through the window slit, swung out as they lowered him down. His feet touched the surface of the lower roof. As he threw off the loop, the rope whipped aloft, and he went to that crumpled figure.

His journey light showed the sprawled body clearly.

And, as Simon went down on his knee he saw that, in spite of his injuries, Fulk of Verlaine still lived. By some chance the wrecker lord's head turned with infinite and painful effort so that the eyes could meet his gaze.

At that moment of meeting Simon's breath expelled in a hiss. He wanted to cry aloud his repudiation of what he saw there. Pain, yes—and hate. And something which was beyond both pain and hate—an emotion which was not of mankind that Simon knew. He said it aloud: "Kolder!"

This was Kolder, the alien menace in the face of a dying man. Yet Fulk was not one of the "possessed," the walking dead men whom Kolder used to fight its battles, the captives sapped of soul, made to cup within their bodies some enlivening power which clean humanity shrank from. No, Simon had seen the "possessed." This was something else again. Because what had been Fulk was not totally erased; that part which bore pain and hate was growing stronger, and that which was Kolder faded.

"Fulk!" Koris had dropped to the roof, come with a loping stride to join Simon. "I am Koris—"

Fulk's mouth worked, twisted. "I die . . . so will you . . . bog-loper!"

Koris shrugged. "As will all men, Fulk."

Simon leaned closer. "And as will those who are not men also!"

He could not be sure that that remnant of fading Kolder understood. Fulk's mouth worked again, but this time all that burst from his lips was blood. He strove to raise his head higher, but it fell back, and then his eyes were blank of all life.

Simon looked across the body to Koris. "He was Kolder," he said quietly.

"But no—not possessed!"

"No, but still Kolder."

"And of this you are sure?"

"As sure as I am of my own mind and body. Kolder in some manner, but still Fulk also."

"What then have we uncovered here?" Koris was already visualizing horrors beyond. "If they have other servants among us beside the possessed—!"

"Just so," Simon replied grimly. "I would say that the Guardians must know of this and that speedily!"

"But the Kolder can not take over any of the Old Race," Koris observed.

"So we shall continue to hope. But Kolder was here, and may be elsewhere. The prisoners—"

Again Koris shrugged. "Of those there are not too many, perhaps a dozen after that last battle in the hall. And they are mainly men-at-arms. Would Kolder pick such for its servants, save as possessed? Fulk, yes—he would be an excellent piece on their playing board. But look you at these and then tell us—if you can."

Sun was a thick bar across the table. Simon fought the need for sleep, finding in his smoldering anger a good weapon in his struggle. He knew her, this gray-robed woman with her hair netted severely back from her rather harsh features, the cloudy jewel, which was her badge of office and sword of war, resting on her breast, her hands folded precisely before her. Knew her, though he could not give her a name—for no witch within Estcarp had a name. One's name was one's most private possession. Give that too lightly to the play of many tongues and one had delivered one's innermost citadel into possible enemy hands.

"This then is your only word?" He did not try to modify his hardness of voice as he demanded that.

She did not smile, no expression troubled her calm gaze.

"Not my word, March Warder, nor the word of any one of us, but the *law* by which we live. Jaelithe—" Simon thought he detected a hint of distaste in her voice as she spoke that name—"made her choice. There is no returning."

"And if the power has not departed from her, what then? You cannot say that it is so by merely speaking words!"

She did not shrug, but something in her pose gave him the feeling that she had so dismissed his speech and his anger. "When one has held a thing, used it, then its shadow may linger with one for awhile, even though the center core of it be lost. Perhaps she can do things which are small shadows of what once she could work. But she cannot reclaim her jewel and be again one of our company. However, I think, March Warder, you did not summon a witch here merely to protest such a decision—which is none of your concern."

It snapped down, that unbreakable barrier between the witches and those outside that bond. Simon took tight rein on his temper. Because, of course, she was right. This was no time to fight Jaelithe's battle, this was a time when a plan must move ahead.

He spoke crisply, explaining what must be done. The witch nodded.

"Shape-changing—for who among you?"

"Me, Ingvald, Koris and ten men of the Borderers."

"I must see those who you would counterfeit." She arose from her chair. "You have them ready?"

"Their bodies—"

She displayed no change of countenance at that information, only stood waiting for him to lead the way. They had laid them out at the far end of the hall, ten men selected from among the slain, led by the broken-nosed, scarred leader of the last defense who wore the insignia of an officer. And, a little apart, Fulk.

The witch paused by each in that line, staring intently into the pale faces, fitting them into her memory, with every mark of identification. This was her particular skill, and while any of her sisterhood could practice shape-changing upon the need, only one expert in the process could attempt such with the actual features of a man, instead of just a general disguise.

When she came to Fulk her survey was much longer as she stooped low, her eyes searching his face. From that lengthy examination, she turned to Simon.

"Lord, you are very right. There was more in this man than his own mind, soul, thoughts. Kolder—" The last word was a whisper, a husky sound. "And being Kolder, dare you take his place?"

"Our scheme depends upon Fulk entering Kars," Simon returned. "And I am not Kolder—"

"As any other who might be Kolder would detect," she warned.

"That I must risk."

"So be it. Bring your men for the changing. Seven and three. And send all others from the hall, there must be no disturbing this."

He nodded. 'This was not the first time he had known shape-changing, but then it had been a hurried grasping for quick disguise to get them out of Kars. Now he would be Fulk and that was a different thing altogether.

As Simon summoned his volunteers, the witch was busied with her own preparations, drawing on the stone flooring of the hall two five-pointed stars, one overlapping in part the other. In the center of each she placed a brazier from the small chest her Sulcar escort had carried in for her. And now she was carefully measuring various powders from an array of small tubes and vials, mixing them together in two heaps on squares of fine silk which had lines and patterns woven into their substances.

They could not strip the bodies, lest the stains and rents betray them. But there was plenty more clothing within the castle, and they would use the weapons, belts, and any personal ornaments the dead had worn, to finish off the picture they must present. This was heaped together waiting the end of the ceremony.

The witch cast her squares of silk into the braziers and began a low chant. Smoke arose to hide the men who had stripped and were now standing, one on each star point. The smoke mist was thick, wreathing each man so that he could not believe that there was anything outside the soft envelope about him. And the chanting filled the whole world, as if all time and space trembled and writhed with the rise and fall of words none of them could understand.

As slowly as it had come the smoke mist ebbed, reluctantly withdrawing its folds, returning once again to the braziers from which it had issued. And the aromatic scent which had been a part of it left Simon lightheaded, more than a little divorced from reality. Then he felt the chill air on his skin, looked down at a body strange to him, a heavier body with the slight beginning of a paunch, a feathering of red-gold hair growing on its skin. He was Fulk.

Koris—or at least the man who moved from Koris' starpoint was shorter—they had selected their counterparts from men not too afar from their own physical characteristics; but he lacked the seneschal's abnormal breadth of shoulder, his long dangling arms. An old sword slash lifted his upper lip in a wolfish snarl, enough to show a toothprint white and sharp. Ingvald had lost his comparative youth and had fingers of gray in his hair, a seamed face marked by many years of evil and reckless living.

They dressed in clothing from the castle chests, slipped on rings, neck chains, and buckled tight the weapons of dead men.

"Lord!" One of the men hailed Simon. "Behind you— it fell from Fulk's sword belt. There."

His pointing finger indicated the gleam of metal. Simon picked up a boss. The metal was neither gold nor silver, but had a greenish cast and it was formed in the pattern of an interwoven knot of many twists and turns. Simon searched along the belt and found the hooks where it once must have been fastened, snapped it back into place. There must be no change in Fulk's appearance, even by so small an item.

The witch was returning her braziers to the chest. She looked up as he came to her, studying him narrowly, as an artist might critically regard a finished work.

"I wish you well, March Warder," she told him. "The Power be with you in full measure."

"For those good wishings we thank you, lady. It is in my mind that we shall need all such in this venture."

She nodded. Koris called from the door. "The tide changes, Simon, it is time we sail."

5   RED MORNING

"SIGNAL FLAGS!" One of the knot of men at the prow of the coaster, now being worked by sweeps up the golden river in the early morning, nodded to the flutter of colored strips from a pole on the bank beside the first wharf of Kars.

He who wore a surcoat gaudily emblazoned with a fish, horns on snout and sloping, scaled head against a crimson square, stirred, his hand going to his belt.

"Expected?" He made an important question of that one word.

His companion smiled. "For what we seem, yes. But that is as it should be. It remains to be seen now whether Yvian is ready to welcome his father-in-law per ax with kindness or the sword. We walk into the serpent's open mouth, and that can snap shut before our reinforcements arrive."

There was a low laugh from the third member of the party. "Any serpent closing his jaws upon us, Ingvald, is like to get several feet of good steel rammed up through its backbone! There is this about blank shields —they are loyal to the man who pays them, but remove that man and they are willing to see reason. Let us deal with Yvian and we shall speedily have Kars thus!" He held out a brown hand, palm up and slowly curled fingers inward to form a fist.

Simon-Fulk was wary of Koris' impetuous estimate of the odds. He did not underrate either the seneschal's fighting ability nor his leadership, but he did question this feverish drive which kept the other at the prow of the coaster all the way up river, staring ahead as if his will could add to their speed. Their crew were Sulcarmen who, as merchants, had made this run before and knew every trick of inducing speed, all of which they had brought into action since they had entered the river's mouth.

In the meantime, the main force of the Estcarpian invaders were coming down through the foothills, ready to dash for Kars when the signal came and that signal . . . Simon-Fulk, for the dozenth time since they had boarded the coaster, glanced at the tall basket cage now draped in a loose cover. In it was the Falconer's addition to their party. Not one of the black-and-white hawks which served the tough mountain fighters as scouting eyes and ears and battle comrades—trained not only to report, but also to fly at the enemy in attack, but a bird which could not be so easily recognized as belonging to Estcarp's allies.

Larger than those hawks which rode at Falconer saddle bows, its plumage was blue-gray, lightening to white on the head and tail. Five such had been discovered overseas by Falconers serving as marines on Sulcar ships. And these had been bred and trained now for three generations. Too heavy to serve as did the regular hawks, they were used as messengers, since they had a homing instinct, and the ability to defend themselves in the air.

For Simon-Fulk's purpose this bird was excellent. He did not dare take one of the regular hawks into Kars, since only Falconers used those birds. But this new breed because of its beauty would catch the attention, and it had been trained to hunt, so that Yvian would welcome it as a gift.

Ten men, a bird and a whole city against them. This was a wild and foolish expedition on the face of it. Yet once before four of them had invaded this same Kars and had come out with their lives and more. Four of them! Simon's hand slipped back and forth along the ornaments on Fulk's belt. Three of them now—himself, Koris and somewhere, hidden in those buildings, Loyse. But the fourth? Do not think of her now. Wonder why she had not returned, why she had allowed him to hear secondhand from the witch at Verlaine that her mission had failed. Where was she—nursing that hurt? But she had accepted the cost of marriage between them, had come to him first! Why—

"We have welcomers, Lord!" Ingvald drew Simon's attention to the here and now.

A file of men at arms, surcoated alike with the badge of Yvian—a mailed fist holding aloft an ax—were on the wharf. Simon's fingers closed on his dart gun, the edge of his cloak discreetly veiling that movement. But on a barked order from their officer the waiting squad clapped their bared hands together and then raised them for an instant, palm out and shoulder high, the greeting of a friendly salute. Thus they were welcomed to Kars.

There was another turn out of barehanded, saluting troops at the citadel gate. And, as far as they had been able to judge on their march through the city, life in Kars flowed smoothly, no sign of unease.

But when they had been ushered with the formality of court etiquette into the suite of chambers in the mid-bulk of the citadel, Simon beckoned Ingvald and Koris to a bowed window. The seven they had brought with them from Verlaine remained by the door. Simon indicated them.

"Why here?"

Koris was frowning. "Yes, why?"

"Bottle us all up together," Ingvald suggested. "And if such handling gives us warning, they apparently do not care. Also—where is Yvian, or at least his constable? We were escorted by a sergeant-at-arms, no one of higher rank. We may be in guests' quarters, but they skimp badly on the courtesy."

"There is more wrong than insult for Fulk in this." Simon pulled off the dead man's ornate helm and leaned his head against the wall where a breeze ruffled the heavy forelock of red-gold hair which he had borne from the shape-changing. "To pen us together is a security move. And Yvian has no reason to honor Fulk. But here there is more—" He closed his eyes, tried to make that mysterious sixth sense deliver other than just the warning which had been growing stronger every step he took into the enemy's hold.

"A sending—there is a sending?" Koris demanded.

Simon opened his eyes. Once a sending had brought him into Kars, a dull pain in his head which marched him, hot, cold, hot, down streets and alley ways to Jaelithe's lodging. No, what he was feeling now was not the same as that. This—it drew him forward, yes—but that was not all. He tingled with a kind of anticipation, such as one felt on the verge of taking some irrevocable step. But also it was not altogether concerned with him. Rather as if he now moved on the edge of some action; brushed by it, but not the true focus point.

"No sending," he made belated answer. "There is something here on the move . . ."

Koris shifted the ax on which he leaned. Volt's gift was never far from his hand. But for his entrance into

Kars it had been disguised with leaf foil and paint into the ornament weapon of a lord's constable.

"The ax grows alive," he commented. "Volt—" His voice sank to a whisper which could not reach beyond the window bay. "Volt guide us!"

"We are in the main block," he added more briskly, and Simon knew that Koris was reviewing mentally the plan of Kars' citadel as they had learned it from reports. "Yvian's private chambers are in the north tower. The upper corridor should have no more than a pair of guards at its far end." He moved towards the door of their own suite.

"How so?" Ingvald looked to Simon. "Do we wait or move now?"

They had planned to wait, but this compulsion Simon could sense . . . Perhaps the bold move was the right one.

"Waldis!" One of the men in Verlaine livery looked up alertly. "We have need for a sack of the bird's grain; it was forgotten in the ship—you seek to send a messenger for it."

Simon pulled aside the covering of the hawk's basket. Those bright eyes, not golden as was usual in that breed, but dark, regarded him intently, having in them a measure of intelligence—not human kind—but yet intelligence. He had never given the bird more than passing heed before, but now he watched it closely as he put hand to the fastening of its prison.

The feathered head turned, away from him, to the door of the room, as if the white one also listened, or strove to hear what could not be picked up by any ear. Then the curved beak opened and the bird uttered a piercing scream at the same moment Simon caught it too—that troubling of the very air about them.

Koris stared at Volt's gift. The shallow disguise of foil could not hide the gleam of the ax head, not brilliant as from sunlight on the burnished metal, but as if the

48

weapon had, for an instant, held fire in its substance. And as suddenly that flash was gone.

The wide, white wings of the hawk fluttered and for the second time the bird screamed. Simon unlatched the cage door, held out his wrist and arm as a bridge. The weight of the bird was a burden, it could never have been carried so, but he held steady as it emerged. Then it fluttered over to perch on the back of a chair.

One of the Borderers held back the door and Waldis came in. He was breathing in great panting gasps and his sword was in his hand, the point of it dripping red.

"They have gone mad!" he burst out. "They are hunting men through the halls, cutting them down—"

It could not be Estcarp forces; they had not yet flown their signal! Nothing to do with them—unless something had gone widely wrong. Ingvald caught the boy's shoulder, drew him closer to Simon.

"Who hunts? Who fights?" he demanded harshly.

"I do not know. All of them by their badges are the duke's men. I heard one shout to get the duke—that he was with his new wife—"

Koris' breath hissed. "I think it is time to move." He was already at the door. Simon looked to the bird mantling on the chair back.

"Open the window casement," he ordered the nearest Borderer. He was being rushed, but that turmoil inside him was a sense of time running out. And if there was already trouble within the citadel they had best make use of that. He motioned and the hawk took off, out through the window, setting a straight course for those waiting. Then Simon turned and ran after Koris.

There was a dead man lying face up at the end of the hallway—his face gone loose and blank. And he wore no mail, but the tunic of some official by its richness, the small badge of Yvian's service on one shoulder. Ingvald paused by the body long enough to point out a small rod of office, broken in two as if the dead had used it in a futile attempt to ward off the blow which had cut him down.

"Steward," the Borderer officer commented. But Simon had noted something else, the inset belt about the other's loose over-robe. Three rosettes, each set with a small wink of red gem in their heart. But where the fourth should have been to complete a balanced pattern was another ornament, a twined and twisted knot, the same as on the belt taken from Fulk, which he, Simon, now wore. Some new trick of fashion or—?

But Koris was already well up the stairs leading to the next floor, the path which would take them to Yvian's apartments and Loyse—if they were lucky. This was no time to speculate about belt ornaments.

They could hear uproar now, distant shouting, the clash of arms. Clearly an all-out struggle of some kind was in progress.

A shout from above, demanding. Then the thud of hollow sounding blows. Simon and Koris burst almost together from the stairwell to see men trying to force the door at the far end of the corridor. Two swung a bench as a battering ram, while others of their fellows stood, weapons in hand, waiting for the splintering barrier to give.

"Yaaaah—" No real war cry, but a shattering scream of rage, out of Koris, as if all the impatience and frustration in him was boiling free. With a feline leap he was halfway along the hall. Two of the Karstenians heard him, turned to face this new attack. Simon shot and both went down, one after the other, the darts finding marks. He was never good in cut-and-thrust melee, having come too late to the learning of sword play, and the niceties of ax attack were not for him. But there were few among either the Guard of Estcarp or the Borderers who could equal his marksmanship with dart gun.

"Yaaaaah!" Koris overleaped the first body, fenced the other toppling man with a shoulder. Now Volt's gift was doing bloody work with those at the battering ram.

Taking no heed for his back, Koris brought the ax down upon the door, and then sprawled forward as whatever bar had held it gave way. The swirl of Borderers had overtaken the remaining Karstenians, passed on after a moment of tight fast work, leaving only dead and dying behind.

Koris was already across the room, now snatching at a hanging to uncover a second and narrower stair. He seemed so sure of his objective that Simon followed without question. Another hall above and, halfway down it, a patch of yellow. Koris grabbed at that, and the folds of a travel cloak billowed out. He tossed it from him as he turned to face the only closed door.

There was no bar here. The first peck of the ax sent it crashing open and they looked into a bed chamber where the bed stood denuded of curtains, its coverings ripped and torn, sliding to the floor in an ominously stained muddle. The man whose fingers were still tightly clawed into those coverlets lay face down. But his legs moved feebly as they watched, striving perhaps to lift him again. Koris stalked forward and put hand to the hunched shoulder, rolled him over.

Simon had never seen Yvian of Karsten, but now he did not mistake the harsh jet of chin, the sandy brows which were a bushy bar across the nose. The sleekness of soft living had not altogether wiped away the forceful mercenary who had fought battles to become my lord duke.

He wore only a loose over-robe which had fallen apart at Koris' handling so that the powerful body, seamed with old scars, was bare, save for a wide, wet, red band at his middle His breath came in great sobbing gulps, and with every moment of his arching chest, that band grew wider.

Koris kneeled beside the duke, so that he could look into Yvian's face, meet his eyes.

"Where is she?" It was asked with no outer heat,

merely a determination to be answered. But Simon doubted if any words could now reach Yvian.

"Where—is—she?" Koris repeated. Under his hand the ax moved, catching light from the window, reflecting it into Yvian's face.

It seemed to Simon that the dying man's attention was not for his questioner, but rather centered on that uncanny weapon, long since fashioned by a non-human smith. Yvian's lips moved, shaped a word, and then a second audible enough—

"Volt—" He made an effort which was visible, looking from the ax to him who held it. And there was a kind of puzzlement in his eyes. Koris must have guessed the source of that for he leaned the closer to speak.

"Volt's ax—and I am he who bears it—Koris of Gorm!"

But Yvian's only answer was a ghostly grin, a stretch of lips which matched the slash of his death wound. He struggled to speak a moment later.

"Gorm, is it? Then you will know your masters. I wish them well—hell-cat—"

One hand freed its hold on the covers and he struck up, his closed fist merely touching Koris' jaw before it fell limply back, that last effort having carried him over the final border into the waiting dark.

Save for Yvian they found these chambers bare, nor were the other two entrances unbarred. Koris, who had led that whirlwind search, came back wide-eyed.

"She was here!"

Simon agreed to that, but Yvian's dying words were in his mind. Why had the duke spoke of "your masters" and connected that with Gorm? For Estcarp he would more rightly have said, "your mistresses." All Karsten knew that the council of witches ruled the north. But Gorm had had grim masters—the Kolder! Someone had started the fighting here, and it had not been Estcarp work. Loyse was gone; Yvian given his death wound.

But they had little time to search farther. A band of the duke's guards came seeking their commander and the Borderer needs must fight their way to make a stand elsewhere.

It was late night and Estcarp was indeed in Kars, when Simon slumped in a chair and chewed at a strip of meat, trying to listen to reports, to assess what had been done here.

"We cannot continue to hold Kars," Guttorm of the Falconers slopped wine from a bottle into a cup, his hand shaking with fatigue. He had led the vans which had cut their way in from the north gate and he had been ten hours at the business of reaching where he now sat.

"We never intended to do so," Simon swallowed his mouthful to answer. "What we came here to do—"

"Is not done!" The full thud was Koris' ax punctuating his speech, haft butt against the floor. "She is not in the city, unless they have hidden her away so that even the witch can not sense her, and that I do not believe!"

Ingvald settled a slinged arm with a grimace of pain. "Nor do I. But the witch says there is no trace. It is as if she never was—or now is—"

Simon stirred. "And there is one way of hiding which blanks out the power—"

"Kolder," Koris replied evenly. Simon thought that he already had accepted that dour possibility.

"Kolder," Simon agreed. "What have we learned from our prisoners—that suddenly, shortly after dawn yesterday, within the citadel some of the officers were given messages, all purporting to come from the duke, all definitely ordering them to quietly assemble the men under their command and then move in on each other! Each commander was told that one of his own fellows was the traitor. Could anything cause greater confusion? Then, unable to reach Yvian, even when they were beginning to realize their orders were wrong, the fighting became more intense as the rumor spread that Yvian had been killed by this one or that."

"A cover, and none of our doing," Guttorm stated, "it was only Yvian's own force involved."

"A cover," Simon nodded. "And the only act which might be so covered was Yvian's death. With his forces sadly split, too broken to organize a hunt for any murderer—"

"Maybe not just Yvian," Koris broke in, "maybe also—Loyse!"

"But why?" Frankly that puzzled Simon. Unless—his tired mind moved slowly but it moved—unless Kolder wanted her for bait.

"I do not know, but I shall find out!" Once more the butt of Volt's gift struck the floor with emphatic force.

6 DUCHESS OF KARSTEN

LOYSE SAT on the wide bed with her knees drawn up, her arms clasped around them, her eyes for that naked blade resting before her. What was Aldis' purpose? It could not be that the duke's mistress thought she would lose her power over Yvian. His need for Loyse was one of expediency only. And Aldis who had ruled him so long would not be easily unseated.

But—Loyse's tongue tip ran along dry lips as she remembered. When Jaelithe had been a seeress in Kars months ago, Aldis had come to her secretly, to buy a spell to keep Yvian truly hers. And she must have believed in the necessity and efficiency of that or she would not have come. Then, in that later battle of wills —when the Guardians had used the most potent sendings they could conjure—Aldis (by image) had been the target of Jaelithe's attack. By all the arts of Estcarp certain temporary commands had then been planted in her to use her influence upon Yvian to further the witches' desires.

Now Loyse could not reconcile this present Aldis with the one she had so long thought upon. This Aldis would not have sought out Jaelithe, save for a contest of strengths. Had that been the real purpose of that visit to the witch of Estcarp? No! Jaelithe's own power would have revealed to her any such plan behind Aldis' seeking. She had then come honestly for her love potion.

And it was the truth that Aldis had been put under control for a period at the battle of wills before the taking of Gorm, even though that had been done from a distance and through images only. A failure there, too, Jaelithe would have known immediately.

Loyse gnawed on her lower lip and continued to stare at the dagger. She herself had failed in meeting with the duke's leman—she had been too assured when she should have been simple and bewildered. Somehow she had been turned inside out, assessed, by opposition she must respect—or fear? Aldis was not Aldis as she had expected her to be. And now, Aldis was playing some game of her own, in which she considered Loyse to be a piece to be moved at her pleasure.

Patiently the girl fought down both hot anger and the tinge of fear which followed the facing of that fact. Ostensibly she had been brought out of Estcarp because she was Yvian's wife by ax marriage. What did Yvian gain by her coming? First, what he had wanted from the beginning—Verlaine with its sea-bought treasure, its fortress, its lower harbor which, with the reef knowledge of its men, would give him a fine raiding port from which to prey on Estcarp.

Second, she was of the old nobility, and perhaps that fact might reconcile the aloof houses to Yvian. The tales out of Kars were that he desired to cut old ties with the mercenaries, establish his ducal throne more firmly by uniting with the rulers of the past.

Third—Loyse hugged her knees more tightly—third, her flight from Verlaine, her joining with his enemies in Estcarp, must have been a goad to personal anger and a wound to his self-esteem. And—those few hints from Aldis—perhaps he chewed now upon the fact that she had sworn betrothal with Koris, that she preferred the outcast of Gorm to the Duke of Karsten. Her lips curled; as if there could be any question between them! Koris was . . . Koris! All she had ever wanted or could want in her life!

Three reasons to bring her here, yet behind them she sensed a shadowy fourth. And, sitting there in the gray of dawn, Loyse tried to summon it into the open. Not Yvian's reason, but Aldis? And why she was sure of that she could not have told either, but that it was true she had no doubt at all.

What could be Aldis' reason? To bring her here, frighten her with those threats of what Yvian had in mind for her—and then deliver into her hand a weapon. So that she might turn that against herself, thus disposing for all time of a rival? A surface reason that, but one which did not quite fit. So that Loyse might turn this length of fine polished metal against the duke when he would have his will of her? But Yvian was Aldis' hold on what she wanted—personal power within the duchy! At any rate Aldis' gift must be considered carefully.

Loyse slid from the bed and went to throw open the window shutters, allowing the wind to sweep across her face, freshen her dully aching head. She thought that it might be mountain wind, though it must have crossed long leagues to be from there. There was a harsh strength to it which she needed to beat against her now.

Somewhere they must be on the move—Koris, Simon, Jaelithe. Loyse did not doubt in the least that they were seeking her. But that they could reach into Kars she did not think possible. No—once more her future depended upon her own resources and wits. She went back to the bed and took up the dagger. Aldis' gift might be in some way a trap, but Loyse knew relief as her fingers closed about the weapon's chill hilt.

Her eyelids were heavy, she dropped back against the bed. Sleep . . . she must have sleep. The table across the door once more? But she could not summon the energy to pull away from the bed and place it so. With the mountain freshening the room she slept.

Perhaps it was those months she had spent campaigning in the border mountains, the need to be alert even in sleep, which had given her that guardian sense. Somewhere in the depths of exhaustion a warning sounded, so that Loyse was out of slumber and awake, though she lay for a long moment with closed eyes—listening, striving with every part of her to learn what chanced.

The faint protest of a hinge—the door! Loyse jerked upright amidst the tumbled covers of the bed. There was morning sun from the window she had left open. The rest of the room was dusky with shadows to which her eyes were more accustomed than were those of the man who entered.

Loyse scrambled to the side of the bed, plunged down, ignoring the dais steps, and put the wide expanse of that massive piece of furniture between her and the invader who had turned his back almost contemptuously as he put the key to lock, this time on the inner side of the door.

He was big—as tall as Simon—and his width of shoulder was not lessened by the folds of his loose bedgown. Big and probably as strong as Koris into the bargain. As he turned to face her with that assured leisureliness, she saw he was smiling a little. And to her mind it was a very cruel and evil smile.

In a way he was like Fulk, but with her father's vivid red-gold coloring blurred into drabber sandiness, the clean cut features coarsened, a scar seam along his jaw line adding an ugly touch. Yvian the mercenary, Yvian the undefeated.

Loyse, her back now against the stone wall, thought that Duke Yvian no longer believed that defeat could ever touch *him*. And that complete self-confidence was in itself a daunting thing to face.

He crossed, with no hurry, to the end of the bed and stood watching her, his smile growing broader. Then he bowed with a mockery bolder than that Aldis had used.

"We meet at last, my lady. A meeting too long delayed—at least I have found it so."

He surveyed her with some of the same contempt Fulk had used to batter her in the past.

"A whey-faced stick indeed." Yvian nodded as if confirming a report. "You have naught to pride yourself upon, my lady."

To answer—would that provoke him into action? Or could silence be a small defense? Loyse wavered between two courses. The longer he talked, the more of a breathing space she had.

"Yes, no man would choose you for your face, Loyse of Verlaine."

Was he trying to goad her into some protest or reply? Loyse watched him narrowly.

"Statecraft," Yvian laughed, "statecraft can drive a man to many things which would otherwise knot his stomach in disgust. So I wed you and now I bed you, lady of Verlaine—"

He did not lunge for her as she feared he might, but advanced deliberately. And Loyse, edging away from him along the wall, read his reason in his eyes. The chase and the capture—that inevitable capture—would provide him with amusement. And, she thought, he would prolong his pursuit of her, savoring her fear, faint hopes born from continued evasion, as long as he wished. Then when he tired, the end would come—at his time and on his terms!

So much would she humor him. With the agility she had learned among the Borderers Loyse leaped, not for the locked door as Yvian might have anticipated, but for the surface of the bed. He had not expected that and his clutch at her fell far short. She sprang again, aided in part by the elasticity of the hide lashings which supported the mattress. Her hands caught the cross ties meant to hold the canopy of state and hangings. Somehow she pulled herself up, perched there, drawing sobbing breaths from the effort which left her momentarily weak, but well above Yvian's reach.

He stared at her. No laughter, no smile now. His eyes narrowed as they must through the visor of his war helm as he looked out upon a battle.

No more talking, he was all purpose. But Loyse doubted if he could climb to rake her down. His weight must be almost double hers and the dusty strips on which she crouched were already creaking when she shifted position. After a long moment Yvian must have agreed on that. His fists closed about a heavy poster of the bed and he began to exert strength against that. Wood creaked, dust sifted into the air. The breath came out of Yvian's chest in heavy grunts. He had been softened by good living, but he still had the frame of a man who had killed more than one in camp wrestling.

The post was yielding and now he pulled at it with short jerks, right and left, loosening it in the bed frame while Loyse's frail perch shook back and forth under her, and only the finger-whitening grip she kept on the timbers held her safe. Then, with a splintering crack, the post broke forward and Yvian stumbled back. Loyse was thrown toward the floor. And the man who had regained his balance with a swordsman's quick double step was waiting for her, the grin back on his sweating face.

She threw herself sidewise as she came and this time she had Aldis' gift ready. Her shoulder met the standing post of the bed painfully, but, even as she cried out,

Loyse slashed with the dagger at the hands reaching to crush her. Yvian snarled and dodged that stab. His robe caught in the splintered end of a broken cross piece which sagged across the bed and for a vital second he was a prisoner. He kicked at the girl viciously, but Loyse scrambled to put the bed again between them.

Yvian jerked his arm free. There was a moist white fleck at the corner of his now pinched lips and his eyes . . . Loyse held the dagger breast high and point out, her left arm still numb from the blow against the post. If she had been hampered by skirts she could never have kept out of his hands, but in riding clothes she was limb free and as agile as any boy. Sword play she knew in part, but knife fighting was an unlearned art. And she was facing a man not only proven in battle, but lessoned in every kind of rough-and-tumble known to blank shields.

He snatched up a draggled sheet from the bed and snapped it at her viciously as a drover would snap a whip. The edge cut her cheek, brought a second cry of pain out of her. But though she gave ground, she did not drop her weapon. Again Yvian lashed at her, and followed that by a lunge, his arms out and ready to engulf her wholly.

It was the table which saved her then. She half fell, half slipped about its end, while Yvian came up against it, taking the full force of that bruising meeting on his thigh, the jar of it slowing him. He found the loose robe hampering and suddenly stopped, fumbling with its belt, striving to throw it off.

His eyes widened, set in a stare aimed across Loyse's hunched shoulder. That device was so old—Loyse's mouth twisted wryly—did he think to catch her in so simple a net? So thinking she was unprepared for the fierce grip which caught her upper arm, pulling her back. There was a strong musky scent, a softness of silken robe against her wrist. Then a white hand slipped down her arm, twisted the knife from Loyse's hand as if she had no strength at all.

"So you had not the nerve to kill." Aldis' voice. "Well, let one who has use this!"

Yvian's amazement was now a black scowl. He stood away from the table to take a quick stride forward. Then he stumbled, gathered balance and came on, in spite of the steel in his middle, the stain growing on his robe. His hands clutched for Loyse. She summoned up the last of her strength to thrust him away. Surprisingly that shove from her made him stagger back and fall against the bed, where he lay tearing at the covers.

"Why—?" Loyse looked at Aldis where she now stood bending over Yvian, watching him with a compelling intentness as if willing him to show any remaining signs of opposition. "Why—?" Loyse could get out no more than that one word.

Aldis straightened, went to the half-open door. She paid no attention to Loyse, her attitude was one of listening. Now the girl could hear it, too—a pounding somewhere below, muffled shouts. Aldis retreated with swift running steps and her hand was again about Loyse's wrist, but this time not to disarm but to pull the girl with her.

"Come!"

Loyse tried to free herself. "Why?"

"Fool!" Aldis' face was thrust close to hers. "Those are Yvian's bodyguards breaking in below. Do you want them to find you here—with him?"

Loyse was dazed. Aldis had thrown the knife which had wounded the duke, and his bodyguard were striving to force their way into his chambers. Why and why and why? Because she could read no meaning into any of this, she did not resist again as Aldis dragged her to the door. The Karstenian's whole body expressed the need for haste, the unease. And to know that Aldis shared fear made it worse for Loyse. To know the enemy was one thing, to be totally caught up in chaos was infinitely worse.

They were in a small hall and the shouting below was louder. Aldis pulled her on into the facing chamber. Long windows opened upon a balcony and Loyse caught glimpses of luxurious furnishings. This must be Aldis' own room. But the other did not pause. Onto the balcony they went and there faced a plank set across to a neighboring balcony on the opposite wall. Aldis pushed Loyse against the railing.

"Up!" she ordered tersely, "and walk!"

"I cannot!" The plank hung over nothingness. Loyse dared not look down, but she sensed a long drop.

Aldis regarded her for a long moment and then brought her hand up to her breast. She gripped a brooch there as if gaining by that touch additional strength to rule Loyse by her will.

"Walk!" she snapped again.

And Loyse discovered that it was as it had been with Berthora, she was not in command of her body any more. Instead, that which was she appeared to withdraw into some far place from which that identity watched herself climb to the plank and walk across the drop to the other balcony. And there she remained, still in that spell, while Aldis followed. The Karstenian pushed aside their frail bridge so that it fell out and down, closing the passage behind them.

She did not touch Loyse again, there was no need to. For the girl could not throw off the bonds that held her to Aldis' desire. They went together through another room and then into a wider chamber. A wounded man crawled there on his hands and knees. But, his head hanging, he did not see them as Aldis swept her captive on, both of them running now.

Loyse saw other wounded and dead, even the swirl of small fighting groups, but none took any notice of the two women. What had happened? Estcarp? Koris, Simon—had they come for her? But all those they saw

locked in combat were Karsten badges, as if the forces
of the duke had split in civil war.

They reached the vast kitchens, to find those deserted, though meat crackled on the spits, pots boiled
and pans held contents which were burning. And from
there they came through a small courtyard into a garden
of sorts with straight rows of vegetables and some trees
already heavy with fruit.

Aldis pulled the long skirt of her outer robe up over
her forearm as she ran. Once she stopped when a tree
branch caught in her jeweled hair net, to break it, but a
portion of the twig still stuck out of the net. That she
had a definite goal in mind Loyse was sure, but what it
might be she did not know until they were splashing
among reeds at the borders of a stream. There was a
skiff there and Aldis motioned to it.

"Get in, lie down!"

Loyse could only obey, the wash of water wetting
through her breeches, over the tops of her boots. Aldis
scrambled in and the skiff rocked with her movements
as she huddled beside Loyse, pulling over the both of
them a musty smelling strip of woven rushes. Moments
later Loyse felt the boat move ahead, they were being
pulled along by the current, probably toward the river
dividing Kars.

The smell of the matting was faintly sickening, and
the water washing in the bottom of the boat had a swamp
stench to it. Loyse longed to lift her head and breathe
clean air again. But there was no disobeying Aldis' orders. Her mind might rage, but her body obeyed.

As the skiff bobbed on Loyse heard sounds which
meant they had reached the river. Now where was Aldis
going? When she had ridden with Berthora she had accepted all their actions as right and normal, had been
so ensorcelled that she had not feared or understood
what she was doing. But this time she knew that she
was under a spell which would make her do just as

Aldis wished. But why—why for everything which had happened to her?

"Why?" Aldis' voice soft close to her ear. "You ask why? But now you are duchess, my lady, all this city, all the countryside beyond is yours! Can you understand what that means, my little nothing out of nowhere at all?"

Loyse tried, she tried very hard to understand but she could not.

There came a hail and Aldis sat up, the matting falling away so that the river air was on them. The rounded side of a ship rose not too far away, and Aldis was reaching for a rope tossed to them from that vessel.

7 THE HIGH WALLS OF YLE

SIMON SAT in the bowed window, his back to the room and those it held. But he could hear—the panther-pacing of Koris, the men reporting, receiving orders, departing again. This was the nerve center of the Estcarpian invasion force and beyond was the city they had taken in an audacious leap and so precariously held. That they continued to so hold it was rank folly, but whether Koris could be made to accept that truth Simon had some doubts. If the seneschal's present mood continued he might try pulling apart the very stones of the buildings, searching for what he would not admit was gone.

Could he blame Koris for this present single-mindedness which was like to imperil their whole cause? Objectively, yes. A half year ago Simon would have witnessed but not understood the torment which tore the younger man now. But since then he had taken to himself his own demons. Perhaps he did not snarl and pace, pounce upon all comers with a demand for news.

However their cases differed in this much: Koris had been bereft by the enemy of what he had come to treasure most; Jaelithe had gone from Simon by her own will, gone and not returned. And by that he was forced to gauge the depth of the rift which had opened between them. Would she have been content had she not awakened to that shadow of power days ago? Or had that return in part of what she had once had brought home to her the loss as she had not realized it, even when she surrendered her jewel upon their marriage? Simon fought his own thoughts, strove to batter them away and consider the problem at hand—that Kars was theirs for a space, that Yvian lay dead, and that Loyse was gone, and no man they had captured knew the manner of her going.

Estcarp and Kars—the problem to hand—and Koris not able to think straight while in his present mood. Simon came away from the window, to step in the path of Koris' pacing and catch the other's arm.

"She is not here. So we look elsewhere. But we do not lose our heads." Simon put snap in that with a purpose, trying to make his voice serve as might a slap across the face of a man caught in hysterical shock.

Koris blinked, broke Simon's hold with a roll of shoulder. But he had stopped pacing, he was listening.

"If she had run—" he began.

"Then perhaps she would have been seen," Simon agreed. "Think now: why would she have been taken? We come to this place and find that mischief was made among the duke's men. And that purpose could have been the death of Yvian or—"

"Some other reason." The voice made them both turn to face the witch who had ridden in with the Borderers. "For another reason," she continued, almost as if she were clearing her thoughts by putting them into words.

"Do you not see, my lord captains, with Duke Yvian dead, his duchess has some claim to Karsten, especially since Loyse is of the old nobility and those clans would rally behind her. They would put her in rule so that they might use her as a shadow screen to cover their own power. This was all done by purpose, but whose purpose? Who is missing—from among the slain, from your prisoners? It would be better not to ask who is dead and why, but who is gone, and the why of that?"

Simon nodded. Good sense—bring Loyse to Kars, confirm her before the duchy as Yvian's consort—with Yvian, perhaps, knowing only a portion of that and believing that portion to be his own plan—and then, dispose of Yvian, use Loyse as a puppet to establish another rule. But which one of the nobles had so devious a mind, such a smoothly running organization as to make it work? As far as Borderer intelligence knew and that was, or Simon had thought it was, very thorough, there was none among the five or six leading families who had either the courage or the ability to set such a complicated plot in action. Yvian would not have trusted any of the once powerful clans to the point that any of their members could have operated so freely within his citadel. And Simon said as much.

"Fulk was not wholly Fulk," the witch replied. "There may be those here who are not wholly what they seem!"

"Kolder!" Koris pounded the fist of one hand into the open palm of the other. "Always Kolder!"

"Yes," Simon replied wearily. "We could not believe that they would give up the struggle with the fall of Sippar, could we? Manpower—or its lack—did we not long ago think that perhaps their greatest weakness? It may be that they can no longer process their possessed armies—at least not here—that what we captured at Gorm has seriously weakened them. If that be so, they may have decided to substitute quality for quantity in their forces, taking over key men—"

"And women!" Koris interrupted him. "There is one

whom we should have found here that we have not seen—Aldis!"

The witch was frowning. "Aldis answered to the sending in the Battle of Power before the assault on Gorm. It may be that thereafter she had no place in Kars."

"There's one way to find out!" Simon strode to where Ingvald sat at a table recording data on a small voice machine the Falconers had brought, a refinement of those carried by their hawks on aerial scouts.

"What mention has there been of the Lady Aldis?"

Ingvald half smiled. "More than a little. Three times those messages which set these wolves at each other's throats were delivered by that lady. And she, being who she was in Yvian's confidence, they took her words as sober truth. Whatever coil was woven here that one had a hand deep in its spinning."

The witch had followed Simon across the chamber and now she rubbed her hands together, between their palms the smoky gem of her profession.

"I would see the private chamber of this woman," she said abruptly.

They went in a body—the witch, Simon, Koris, and Ingvald. It was a dainty bower and a rich one, opening from the same upper hall as that room in which they had discovered the dying Yvian. At the room's end long windows opened upon a balcony and the wind stirred the silken curtains of the bed, fluttered a lace scarf drifting from a chest. There was a musky scent which sickened Simon and he went to the open windows.

The witch, her gem still tight between her palms, walked about the room, her hands well out from her at breast level. What she was doing Simon could not guess, but that it had serious meaning he knew. Those hands passed over the bed, down its full length, swept across the two chests, the mirrored toilet table with its assortment of small boxes and vials carved from polished stones. Then, in mid-passage over that array, the clasped hands hesitated, poised hawk fashion, and came down in a swoop, though nothing lay below that Simon could see.

She turned to face the men. "There was a talisman here—a thing of power which had been used many times—but not our power. Kolder!" She spat that in disgust. "It is a thing of changing—"

"Shape-changing!" Koris cried. "Then she who seemed to be Aldis might not be her at all!"

But the witch shook her head. "Not so, lord captains! This is not the matter of shape-changing which we have long used, this is a changing within, not without. Did you not tell me that Fulk was not Fulk, and still not completely possessed? He was different in that he fled battle where once he would have led his men to the end. But he ran to protect that which was in him, choosing to fall at the last to his death rather than be taken by you while it was a part of him. So will this woman be. For it is firm in my mind that she also carries that inside her which is from Kolder."

"Kolder," Koris repeated between set teeth. Then his eyes went wide and he said that word with a different inflection altogether. "Kolder!"

"What—?" Simon began, but Koris was already continuing.

"Where is the last stronghold of those cursed man stealers? Yle! I tell you—this thing which was once Aldis has taken Loyse and they head for Yle!"

"That's only guessing," countered Simon. Though, he added silently, it was a logical guess. "And even if you are right, Yle's a long way from here, we have good chance to intercept them." And so an excellent reason for prying you out of Kars before disaster is upon us, again he added mentally.

"Yle?" The witch visibly considered that.

Simon waited for an added comment. The witches of Estcarp were no mean strategists, if she had some contribution to make it would be to the point and worth listening to. But, save for that one word, she was silent. Only her gaze went from Koris to Simon and back as if she saw something that neither man could sense. However, she did not speak, and there was no chance of getting it from her by questioning, as Simon knew of old.

That Koris might be right they had proof before moonrise. Not wishing to linger in Kars, the raiders had withdrawn to the ships in the harbor, commandeering transports to take them west to the sea. The sullen crews worked under the guard of Estcarpian forces with a Sulcar commander in each ship.

Ingvald led the rearguard onto the last of the round-bellied merchant vessels and stood with Simon, looking back at the city where the whirlwind, partly of their making, had hit a day earlier.

"We leave a boiling pot behind us," the Borderer commented.

"Since you are of Karsten, would it have been more to your mind to stay to tend this pot?" Simon asked.

Ingvald laughed harshly. "When Yvian's murderers fired my garth and sent their darts into my father and brother, then did I swear that this was no land of mine! We are not of this new breed in Kars and it is better for us that we ride now with Estcarp, since we are of the Old Race. No, let this pot be tended now by who wills. I hold with the Guardians in the thought that Estcarp wants no land or rule beyond her own borders. Look you—do we strive to make Karsten ours now? Then we needs must stamp out a hundred rebel fires down the full length of the duchy. And to do that we should strip the northern keeps. For that Alizon waits—

"We have rid this city of Yvian, the strong man who crested its rule for long. Now will there be five, six of the coastwise lords tearing at each other's flanks to take his place. And, so embroiled, they will have no mind to trouble the north for a space. Anarchy here serves our cause better than any occupation force."

"Lord!" Simon turned as the Sulcar captain of the ship came up. "I have one here with a story. He thinks it worth selling, perhaps he is right."

He shoved forward a man wearing the grimed and stained clothing of a common sailor, who promptly bent knee in the servility of Yvian's enforcement.

"Well?" Simon asked.

"It is thus, lord. There was this ship. She was a coaster, but not of the usual order. Her men, they did not go ashore, though she was dock set for two days, maybe three. And they sent no cargo to the wharves, nor did they ride hold-filled when they came in So we watched her, m' mate and me. And we saw naught, save that she was so quiet. But when the fighting started in the city, then she came to life. The men, they take out their sculls and cast off. But so did a lot of others, so that was not so different. Only all the others they kept goin' once they started—"

"And this ship did not?" Simon could not see the purpose, but he had confidence enough in the Sulcar captain's recommendation to listen the tale out.

"Just to over stream—" The sailor nodded to the opposite bank of the river, keeping his eyes respectfully on the deck planking. "There they sat on their sculls while the rest of those on the run headed up river. Then there was this boat, a small skiff just drifting along—like lost from a tow. But they did some fast sculling to get it on the port side where it was hid. And it didn't come out again. Only after that they were on the move, headin' downstream instead of up."

"And you thought that odd?" Simon prompted.

"Well, yes, seein' as how your men were coming from that direction. O' course most of them were ferried across the river by then and hittin' the city. Maybe those others—they thought a try at gettin' back down to the coast was better than headin' inland on the river."

"Picked someone up from the skiff," Ingvald said.

"So it would seem," Simon agreed. "But who? One of their own officers?"

"This skiff now," the Sulcar captain took a hand in the questioning, "who did you see aboard her?"

"That's what makes it so queer, sir. There weren't nobody. Course we did have no seein' glass on her, but all that showed above the gunnel was a piece of reed mat. There weren't nobody rowing or even sittin' up in her. Was they anybody on board, they was lyin' flat."

"Injured in the fighting?" Ingvald speculated.

"Or simply in hiding. So this ship then headed for the seacoast, down river?"

"Yes, lord. And that there's queer, too—how she went, I mean. They was men standin' to her sculls right enough—only they was like makin' a play of it, just like the current was runnin' so fast they didn't need to do any more'n maybe just fend her off from some sandbank now and then. There's a current here, sure, but not as strong as that. You need scullin' if you want to make time and the wind's in the wrong quarter—which it was then. But they was makin' time—good time."

The Sulcar captain looked across the bowed head of the seaman to Simon. "I do not know of any way save sculls or wind to move in the river," he reported. "If a ship has such a method of travel, then that kind of ship I have not seen before, nor have any of my brothers. The wind and oars we know, but this is—magic!"

"But not of the Estcarpian kind," Simon replied. "Captain, make signal to the seneschal's ship. Then put me aboard her with this man also."

"Well, Captain Osberic," Koris turned to the Sulcar fleet commander when the story had been repeated to him, "is this a tale poured from some wine bottle, or could it be true?" That he wanted to believe that it was true, had already fitted it into his own quest, was apparent to them all.

"We know of no such vessel—that this man saw what

he has told us, yes, that I believe. But there are ships which are not ours."

"This was no submarine," Simon pointed out.

"Perhaps not, but as they seem to copy now our shape-changing, perhaps Kolder might give another covering to a vessel as well. Perhaps in the confusion existing along the river while we were setting our men across, they took a chance on betraying their alienness to gain time they believed they needed."

Koris slipped the haft of Volt's gift up and down in his hand. "Down river to the sea, then to Yle."

Only perhaps, Simon wanted to remind him. If the ship, small as it must have been to resemble the river craft, was really more than it seemed, it could be heading to Yle—or even overseas to the Kolder nest which lay no man knew where.

But Koris had already made up his mind. "The fastest ship you have, Osberic, our men for the sculls if need be. We're going after."

Only if the ship was ahead of them, it had made good use of its long head start. With night a wind came to fill the sail Osberic had set, and they slipped along at as smart a clip as any river vessel knew, not needing scull labor. Behind them the string of transports was nosing into the northern shore, to disembark the raiders who would ride for the border, leaving chaos behind them. Only Osberic's chosen ship and two others, with Sulcar crews pursued the river chase.

Simon had some hours of sleep, his cloak about him, the discomfort of Fulk's mail still heavy on his limbs. They had rid themselves of their shape-changed disguises, but the borrowed weapons and clothing they still wore. His sleep was uneasy, full of dreams which fell to fragments each time he awoke, though he was plagued with the thought that they were important. And at last he lay watching the stars, listening to the wind, and now and then the murmur of some Sulcar man on duty. Koris lay an arm's length away and Simon thought that perhaps fatigue had struck at last and the seneschal slept.

Yle—and Kolder. There would be no turning Koris aside from Yle—short of putting him in bonds by force. Yet, there was taking Yle either. Had they not bit again and again on that hard nut these past months? They had won into Gorm because chance had taken Simon as a prisoner into that stronghold and made him aware of certain chinks in Kolder armor. But then Kolder had been confident, almost contemputous of its opponents with their vulnerability to Kolder might.

The enemies' defeat in Sippar would have taught them a lesson. Had in this much—that there was now an invisible barrier about Yle by both land and sea—a barrier nothing, not even the power of the witch probe, could pass. For months Yle had been sealed. If the garrison of that stronghold came or went, it was by sea, and not on the surface of that sea. The Kolder ships were submarines, three such had been taken at Gorm. But—

Simon knew again the doubts which had moved him months earlier when he had stood before the Council of Guardians and had given the opinion they had asked for: leave the things found at Gorm alone, be very careful of the alien secrets lest they unleash something they could neither understand nor control. Had he been wrong then? He wavered now. Yet something inside him still argued firmly that he was right, to use Kolder means was to deliver oneself in part to the enemy.

That the witches were exploring the finds on Gorm slowly, carefully, Simon knew. And that did not disturb him, for they would use every possible safeguard, and their own power was a barrier which Kolder recognized. But to put into the hands of others those machines . . .

Yet they might have a way there of breaching Yle now. Simon had thought of it before, but never, not even to Jaelithe, had he put that thought into words.

It might be that he alone could once more crack the shell of a Kolder fortress. Not via submarine—he had not the knowledge for that, and they had not yet discovered what motive force propelled those ships, unless it could be the mental power of the Kolder leader who had died with the metal cap on his head, failing his men at the last. No, not under the sea, but through the air. Those flyers lined up on the roof top in dead Sippar—they might be the key to Yle. But to mention that to Koris would be the rankest folly.

8 *PRINT OF KOLDER*

"It is locked tight—" The curved blade of Volt's gift bit into the thick green turf viciously as Koris would have used it against the enemy. They stood on the heights looking across the seaward valley to Yle.

Gorm had been ravaged from the people of this time and world. But in Yle the Kolder had built on their own. One would, Simon thought, have expected them to raise towers and walls of metal. But they had used the stone common to Estcarpian architecture, the only difference being that buildings throughout the witch land were old, old with the seeming of having been born from the very bones and flesh of the earth which based them, rather than built by men. And this Yle, for all its archaic stone, was new. Not only new, but divorced from the soil and rock about it in a way Simon could feel, but not put into words. He believed that even if he had not known that this was a Kolder hold, he would have realized that it was not of Estcarp or any neighbor nation.

"There was a door there—" Koris pointed with his ax to the face of the now smooth wall below and a little to the right. "Now even that is gone. And no one can get an ell closer than that stream in the valley."

The barrier, much like the one which had kept all intruders out of Gorm, held them now from any closer investigation of the alien pile. Simon stirred uneasily. There was a way. That kept nibbling at his mind through the days since they had left Kars, until he was at war with himself.

"They must enter or leave under the sea, as they did in Gorm."

"So do we turn our backs now and say we are beaten; Kolder has won? That I do not say, not while breath fills my lungs and I have arm strength to swing this!" Once again the ax sliced turf. "There is a way— there must be!"

What pushed Simon then to say what he had sworn to himself that he would not? But the words almost spoke themselves.

"There might be a way—"

Koris whirled, his ungainly body in a half crouch as if he fronted an adversary in a duel.

"By sea? How can we—?"

Simon shook his head slowly. "Remember the fall of Sulcarkeep," he began, but Koris took the words from him.

"By air! Those flying ships at Sippar! But how can we use them, not knowing their magic." His bright eyes demanded things of Simon. "Or do you know that magic, brother? In your tales of your own world you have spoken of such as an aid in your wars. To turn their own weapons against this scum—aha—that would be a good hosting! Aiiiii!" He tossed the great ax into the air and caught it by the haft, his head up so that the sun struck full on his face. "To Gorm then—for these flying ships!"

"Wait!" Simon caught at Koris' arm. "I am not even sure we can fly them."

"If they can be flown to crack this viper den, then we shall do it!" Koris' nostrils were pinched, his mouth a forbidding seam above the grim line of his jaw. "I know that to use alien magic is a chancy thing, but there comes a time when a man grasps all or any weapons to give him aid. I say we go to Sippar and get what we must have."

Simon had not been back to the horror which was Gorm's chief city for months. He had had no desire to be one of those who had combed the buildings which were tombs for the deluded islanders who had welcomed Kolder to aid in a dynastic battle. Simon had had enough of Gorm and Sippar in the fighting which had driven Kolder from that snug nest.

Today he discovered that there was another reason beside those old horrors which moved him to hatred for the halls of Sippar. He stood again in what had been the control chamber of that strange network, where the gray-clad Kolder officers had sat at their tables before their installations, all governed by the capped leader, thinking out—Simon was sure—the orders which had motivated all life within the captured citadel. For moments out of time he himself had shared the thoughts of that leader and so learned the source of Kolder—that these aliens like himself had come through some weird door in space and time to this world, seeking a refuge from disaster at their heels. Yes, he had shared the thoughts of Kolder, and now as he stood there again, once more that scrap of another's memory seemed twice as vivid, as real as if even here and now they were joined mind to mind—though that other mind had been many months dead.

But it was not only with the Kolder that Simon had shared in this hall. It was here that the witch of

Estcarp with whom he had shared many ventures had laid aside her jewel, given into his keeping her life, by her standards, when she had spoken her name—that most intimate possession which must not be yielded to another lest power be passed to that other, power over one's innermost self. Jaelithe—

Simon waited for the familiar stab of hurt to follow fast on the heels of memory. But this time it was not so sharp, rather as if between them hung a softening shield of indifference. The Kolder memory was far the keener, and Simon knew, with unease, that Jaelithe's defection had not troubled him with the same urgency since he had come out of Kars. Yet—yet they had held a good thing between them, a true thing—or so he had believed. And the loss of that left a wound which might heal in time, yet the scar would not vanish.

Why? The witch had been explicit at Verlaine. For Jaelithe, no return was allowed. Did she hate him now so that she could not bear to see him? No message even. Kolder! Now was the time to think of Kolder and the confounding of that chill evil, and not of things broken past the mending. Simon concentrated on Kolder.

"Simon!" Koris called from the doorway. "The sky ships—they are as we left them."

Ships for the invasion of Yle. Why had he ever thought it wrong to use their own weapons against the enemy? Why did he see danger lurking in the alien machines? Of course Koris was entirely right in this matter. To crack the shell of Yle what better hammer than those its builders had devised?

They climbed to the roof where stood the flyers. Two had been in the process of being repaired, parts and tools still laid out by workmen who had vanished. Simon went straight to the nearest. But this was simple—there was no need to worry about getting it into action again. One did this and this, tightened this . . .

He was working with confidence, some part of his brain directing every movement of his hand, as if conning a detailed chart. Simon slipped the last fitting into place, then climbed into the cockpit, thumbed the starter button, felt the vibration purr. It was all right, he could lift.

A shouting below, loud, and then dying into the distance as the flyer took off. Simon adjusted the controls. Yle, he was bound for Yle—a task of importance waiting him. The barrier could not hold much longer; there had been too many calls upon the central energy. Sooner or later the barbarians would breach it. The pound of the power of these cursed hags would then shake the walls down.

Cursed hags? Yes, tricky, evil all of them! Wed a man and then walk away from him without a backward look, deeming him too stupid to hold to. Hag—hag!

Simon made a song of that word as he flew over the waters of the bay. Gorm—they had lost Gorm. Perhaps they would lose Yle—for now. But the plan was working. Ah, yes, just let the gate be opened and the great energy tapped, then these stupid savages, those hags would meet with a reckoning! Sippar's fall would be nothing to what would happen in Es. Push here, pull there, move a savage to action, ring in the hags with trouble. Win time—time was what was needed— time for the project at the gate.

So give up Yle now if need be. Let the barbarians believe they had won again, that Kolder was driven away. But Kolder would only withdraw to its source, to wax stronger again—then to move, renewed, straight into the heart of opposition—Es itself!

Simon blinked. Under his confidence, this new and heady knowledge of what was to be done and why, there was a writhing discomfort, as if a fighter held down a still struggling opponent he could not quite master. Ah, there was Yle. And they would be waiting. They had known, they had sumoned—and now they waited!

His hands moved on the controls though he was not

really conscious of any need for those movements. Flashes inland—the barbarian forces. His mouth shaped a sneer. All right, let them have their worthless triumph here. By the time they broke in with the aid of the hags there would be nothing left worth the gaining. Down now; he must set down on this roof.

The landing gear touched cleanly. For a moment Simon looked about dazedly. This—this was Yle! How had he come here? Koris, the forces . . . His head turned— no, this was true, no dream. He sat alone in a Kolder flyer from Sippar! There was pain in his head, a sickness in his middle. His hand fell from the controls, his fingers without his orders went to Fulk's sword belt, touched a boss there, began to trace its curves and indentations.

Yes, this was Yle and his task was only beginning. They were coming now, those he must take from this place before it fell to the hags and their savages. A square opened in the roof and from that emerged a rising platform bearing two women. That one—she would give the orders—she was the one who had worked so ably to further the plan in Kars. And the one walking under full control by her side—she was the pawn to be played!

Simon pushed open the cabin door and waited, still in the pilot's seat. Loyse—again that stir under the surface within him, but less now, more easily pushed aside. She was staring at him, her eyes wide and wild, but she was under control, they would have no trouble with her. Already she had settled as ordered in the seat behind him. Now that other—Aldis. Aldis?

"To sea."

He did not need that order from her. Simon was pricked by irritation. He knew as well as she where they must fly. They spiraled into the air.

Odd. Mist growing thicker. Aldis leaned forward from beside her charge, eying that gathering cloud outside the cabin as if in fear. And she was right—this was some devilment of those hags. But they could not control the flyer, nor turn him from his course, even though they could bewilder his eyes . . . his eyes . . .

Simon stared. Something white moving on the course of the flyer, keeping pace effortlessly, a little above and ahead. Of course, that was his guide—just keep with that and he need not worry about the mist. They flew on but there seemed no end to the fog which enclosed them. The hags fought hard, only they could not control the flyer. Men they might bend to their purposes but not machines, never the machines! With machines one could be sure—be safe!

The mist was more than blinding, it was confusing, too. Perhaps it was not wise to stare into its eddying mass. But if he did not he would lose sight of that white guide. . . . What was it! Simon could not make it out clearly, always some tendril of the mist blurred its outline when he stared intently.

On and on. In the mist time was distorted, too. Some more of their so-called "magic." Ah, they were artful in deceit all those witches!

"What are you doing?" Aldis leaned forward, her gaze now on one of the dials among the controls. "Where are we going?" Her voice was louder and shriller with that second demand.

"What is ordered." Simon was again irritated by the necessity for answering her. She had done good work, this female, but that was not to say that she had any right to question *him*, his competence, his actions.

"But this is not the course!"

Of course it was! He was obeying orders, following his guide. How dared she say that?

Simon looked down at the dial. Then his hand went to his head. Dizzy—he was dizzy. No need to look at the dials—just follow the white guide, that would make all right. "Be quiet!" he flung at the woman behind him.

But she would not. Now she pulled at his arm. "This

is not the way!" She screeched that until her voice hurt his ears. His seat behind the controls was too cramped to let him turn far. But he thrust at her with his right hand pushing her back and away.

She fought back, striving to get at him, her nails raking at the flesh across the back of his hand, and he feared to lose course, have the white guide hidden by the thick enclosure of the mist. A back-hand push made her gasp and flinch and Simon's attention was again for that half-seen thing ahead.

Only now he did see it fully—just for an instant. A bird—a great white bird! A white bird! He had known a white bird before—and the mist left his mind. The white hawk, that trained messenger they had carried into Kars—into Kars . . .

Simon twisted, a small choked cry forced out of him. Kolder! Kolder influenced thoughts, leading him— He stared down at his hands on the controls, totally ignorant now of what they must do, of how to keep the flyer aloft. Panic was a sharp, sick taste in his mouth. Somehow he had been used. His left hand groped down hunting—hunting what? Fascinated Simon watched that movement he had not consciously willed. The fingers touched Fulk's belt, slipped swiftly along to that entwined knot of green metal which did not match the other bosses. That!

Now he did use his will to pull his hand away—a struggle which left him sweating. He turned his head. Aldis' hands were tight to her breast, she eyed him with a dark hate, but under that—was it fear?

Simon caught one of her slim wrists, pulled her hand away from what it sought to conceal. Her other hand clung the tighter, but he caught a glimpse of glinting green. Whatever strange talisman had been Fulk's, Aldis wore its match. His own hand jerked, twitched, he could hardly keep it away from the belt ornament.

Under them the flyer lurched, dived through the mist. If he did not replace his hand he would not be able to pilot them safely, that much Simon guessed. But he would also return to the bondage which had made him serve Kolder. To crash might mean all their deaths. To accept Kolder control at least postponed that for a space, and time might fight on his side. Simon no longer resisted. His fingers flashed to the intricately carved bit of metal, traced its pattern.

He was—where? What had happened? Tricks, the hag tricks—they had befuddled him. No more, no more of those!

A scream—not from any human throat. Coming straight at the cabin window, as if to fly into his face, that bird, its cruel beak open. Simon's hands flew to the controls in reflex action, striving to pull under that determined attack. Out of the curls of mist a shadow—a red shadow which took on too much substance. The flyer sideswiped that, the machine spinning from impact. Aldis' screams were louder and shriller than the hawk's. Simon cursed as he fought for control. They were still airborne but he could not bring them up, gain any altitude. Sooner or later they were going to land and the best he could do was to try to touchdown under power.

Simon fought the stubborn machine for that slim chance. They struck, a surface still hidden in a blinding mist—bounced—set down again. Simon's head hit the cabin wall and he was not truly aware when they were still, the flyer tilted at an angle, nose down. Mist pushed exploring fingers through the door, now cracked open. And with it came a rank stench, the smell of swamp, overpowering with stagnant water and rotting vegetation. Aldis pulled herself up, looked about, drew a deep, explorative breath of that exhalation of decay. Her head turned as if impelled by some impulse and her hand stirred on the Kolder token.

She leaned forward, but quickly halted that as the flyer rocked. Her hand caught at Simon, pulled off his helm. With a tight finger hold in his thick hair she dragged his lolling head back.

There was a trickle of blood on his left temple, his eyes were closed. But the fact that he must be unconscious seemed to make no difference to the woman. Her grasp on his hair held his head as close to her lips as she could manage. And now she spoke—no words of Karsten, nor of the older dialect of Estcarp—but a series of clicking sounds, more the beat of metal against metal than any human speech.

Though his eyes did not open, his head moved. He pulled feebly against her hold, but she did not yield to his struggle. For the second time she repeated her message. Then she waited. But he did not rouse. When Aldis released her grip his head fell forward on his chest.

The woman gave an exclamation of irritation. She strove for a view outside and was rewarded by sighting the twisted skeleton of a long dead tree, its broken branches hung with wisps of palid moss swaying in the wind. The wind was also driving out the mist, clearing a view which did not lead one to optimism.

Green-scummed water in pools, from which a wood of dead trees protruded, as might skeleton hands raised in threat to the sky, bloated growths anchored to the trees. As she watched, one of those came to life, an obscene lizard-like thing of splotched skin and toothed jaws crawling towards the flyer.

Aldis' hand pressed tight against her mouth. She was trying to think. Where could they be? This country was beyond her knowledge and the knowledge of those she served. Yet, her head again turned to the right—*they* were here—or one who served them was. And that meant help. Her hands cupped about the token, she bent all her forces into a summons.

9 TORMAN'S LAND

SIMON OPENED his eyes. The pain in his head seemed one with the greenish light about him. He moved and what supported him responded by rocking in a way which was a warning even his dimmed consciousness could understand. He looked up—to face nightmare!

Only the transparent shell of the cabin window kept that toothed horror from him. Its claws raked the surface of the flyer as it lumbered across the nose of the machine. Unable to move Simon followed that slow progress with his eyes. It had some vague resemblance to a lizard, but its bulk and awkward movements were unlike the eagle litheness of those creatures as he had seen them in his own world. This thing had a leprous, warty skin, as if it had been striken by some foul disease. Now and then it paused to view him, and there was a malignity in those large whitish eyes which gave terrifying purpose to its deliberate advance.

Simon turned his head with care. The door was open, sprung by the crash. A few more feet, and a little maneuvering by the lizard thing, and it would achieve its goal. He moved his hand by inches, drew the dart gun from his belt holster. Then he remembered the women. With all the care he could muster, Simon changed position, the flyer rocking. The lizard hissed, seemed to spit. A milky liquid hit the cabin window, trickled down its cracked surface.

He could not see Loyse who was immediately behind him. But Aldis sat there, her eyes tightly closed, both hands again over the Kolder talisman, her whole

84

tense position testifying to intense concentration. Simon dare not move far enough to reach the door. The flyer seemed balanced on some point and it dipped nose down at any change of the distribution of weight within.

"Aldis!" Simon spoke loudly, sharply—he must break through the web she had woven about herself. "Aldis!"

If she did hear him the urgency of his voice meant nothing. But there was a breathy sigh from behind him.

"She talks with *them*," Loyse's voice, a shadow of sound, worn and weary.

Simon caught at the hope it gave him. "The door—can you reach the door?"

Movement and again the flyer rocked. "Sit still!" he ordered. And then saw that the movement, as dangerous as it had been, had aided them in this much, the lizard thing was slipping, despite all its efforts, down the inclined slope of the flyer's nose. Its claws could not dig into the sleek stuff of the machine's surface.

It opened its mouth and gave voice to a hooting honk as, still scrabbling for a foothold, it went over the edge. On the ground, if the swamp surface could be termed "ground," it might yet find its way to the open door. Simon thought he dared not delay.

"Loyse," he said quickly, "move as far back as you can—"

"Yes!"

The flyer rocked. But the nose was rising, he was sure of that.

"Now!" From the tail of his eye Simon caught a glimpse of hands in action. Loyse was adding to his instructions with an idea of her own as she gripped Aldis by the shoulders and dragged her back in turn. Simon slid along the seat, his hand now on the edge of the open door. But he could not get in the right position to exert much strength and he could not bring it closed.

The flyer rocked violently as Aldis struggled in Loyse's hold, lying back upon the girl who had her in a fierce clutch. Simon struck and the Kolder agent went limp, her hands falling away from the enemy talisman.

"Is she dead?" Loyse asked as she pulled from beneath the limp weight of the other woman.

"No. But she will not trouble us for a space. Here—"

Together they pushed Aldis to the back and that change of weight appeared to establish the flyer so that it no longer swung under them, providing they moved cautiously. For the first time Simon had a chance to survey what lay beyond, though he kept watch on the door, his gun ready.

The half-immersed, dead wood, the scummed pools, and weird vegetation—this was like nothing he had seen before. Where they were he had no idea, nor could he tell clearly how they had come here. The stench of the swamp was in itself a deadening thing which clogged lungs and added to the pain in his head.

"Where is this place?" Loyse broke the silence first.

"I don't know—" Yet far in the back of memory there was something . . . A swamp. What did he know of a swamp? Outside the moss on the long dead trees stirred with the dank wind. There was a rustling in a clump of pointed reeds. Reeds . . . Simon frowned with pain and the effort at remembering. Reeds and scummed pools —and a mist—those he remembered from far away and long ago. From his own time and world? No—

Then all at once for a second or two he was an earlier Simon Tregarth, the one who at dawn had come through a gate onto a wild moor under the rain. The Simon Tregarth who had run with a fugitive witch before the hounds of Alizon hunters—and they had skirted just such a bog while the witch had appealed to its indwellers for aid, only to be refused. So they needs must cut across the edge of the swampland and find elsewhere a refuge. The Fens of Tor! Forbidden country which no man save one had been known to enter and return from again. And that man had fathered Koris of Gorm. He had brought his Torwoman out and held her to wife, in spite of his people's hatred and fear of such blood mixing. But the heritage he had so left his son had been sorrow and loss. Tor blood did not mix, the Tor marshes were closed to all outsiders.

"Tor—the Fens of Tor," Simon heard Loyse gasp in answer.

"But—" She put out her hand. "Aldis was calling for aid. And yet Tor does not mix with outworlders."

"What does anyone know of the secrets of Tormarsh?" Simon countered. "Kolder has entered Kars, and I will swear that it walks elsewhere, as in Alizon. Only the Old Race cannot accept the Kolder taint and know it instantly for what it is. That is why Kolder fears and hates them most. Perhaps in Tormarsh there is no such barrier to mingling."

"She called. They will answer—and find us here!" Loyse cried.

"That I know." To go out into that swamp might well mean death, but it held also a thin promise of escape. To remain pent in the crashed flyer would lead but to recapture. Simon wished that his head did not ache, that he knew only a little of where they lay in the swamp. They might be only yards away from the border through which he and Jaelithe had fled. The trees, he decided, provided their best road. For all those which still stood, or leaned, an equal number lay prone, their length in a crazy pattern furnishing at least a footway over the treacherous surface.

"Where will we go?" Loyse asked.

It might be folly, to head into the unknown, but still every nerve in Simon screamed against remaining to be picked up by any force Aldis might have summoned. Slowly he unhooked that belt with its betraying boss. The long dagger and dart gun he would need. He looked at Loyse. She wore riding clothes, but had not even a knife at her belt.

"I do not know," he replied to her question. "Away from this place—and soon."

"Yes, oh, yes!" Carefully she edged about Aldis, balanced to look out the door. "But what of her?" Loyse nodded to the unconscious agent.

"She remains."

Simon looked out below. There were tufts of coarse grass crushed beneath the flyer. The machine had landed on the edge of what might be an islet of solid ground. So far, so good. The grass had been flattened enough so that he thought they need not fear any life lurking in it. Wherever the lizard thing had gone, it had not yet appeared near the door. Simon dropped out, his boots sinking a little into the footing but bringing no ooze of water. Holding out his hands to Loyse, he eased her down and gave a little push towards the rear of the flyer.

"That way—"

Simon pulled at the door, setting the flyer to rocking. But the jammed metal gave as he exerted his full strength. That would shut Aldis in and—well, he could not leave even a Kolder-ruled woman to the things which made this foul country their home and hunting ground.

The ridge of ground on which they had crashed ran back, rising higher. But it was only an island, giving root room to the grass, a bordering of reeds, and some stunted brush. On three sides were murky pools—or perhaps only one pool with varying shallows and deeps. The water was scummed, and where cleared of that filthy covering, an opaque brown beneath which anything might lie in cover. As far as Simon could see the best path out still remained via the sunken tree lengths. How waterlogged and rotted those were was now a question. Would they crumple under the weight of those using them as bridges? There was no way of knowing until one tried.

Simon kept the dart gun, but he handed the knife to Loyse.

"Do not follow on any log until I have already cleared it," he ordered. "We may be only going deeper into this sink, but I do not propose to try the water way."

"No!" Her agreement was quick and sharp. "Take care, Simon."

He summoned up a tired smile which hurt his bruised face. "Be very sure that this is advice I shall hug to me now."

Simon caught a branch of a moss-wreathed tree which stood at the edge of the grass plot. A measure of the ancient bark powdered in his grip, but there remained still a hard core firm to his testing. Holding to that, he swung out, to land on the first of the logs. The wood did not give too much, but bubbles arose in the water, breaking to release so vile a stench that he coughed.

Still coughing he worked his way along to a mass of upended roots where he rested. Not that the mere walking of that way was fatiguing in itself, but the tension in his body had stiffened his joints to make every effort twice as hard. To climb over the roots, find footing again beyond was a task which sapped his strength yet more. He stood there, to watch Loyse come the path he had marked, her pale face set, her body as stiff as his.

How long did it take, that crisscross trailing from log to log? Twice Simon looked back, sure that they must have come some distance, only to see the flyer still far too close to hand. But at last he did leap to another grass-covered ridge, hold out his hands to Loyse. Then they sat together, shivering a little, panting and rubbing the hard muscles of their legs which seemed to have locked during that ordeal.

"Simon—"

He glanced at the girl. Her tongue moved across her lips as she stared at the stagnant water.

"The water—it can not be drunk—" But that was not a statement, it was a question, a hope that he would say she dared. His tongue moved in his own dry mouth as he wondered how long they would be able to stand up to temptation before they were driven by thirst to scoop up what could be rank poison.

"It is foul," he replied. "Perhaps some berries—or a

real spring later on." Very pallid hopes, but they could help to stave off temptation.

"Simon—" Resolutely Loyse had raised her gaze from the slimy pool, was gazing back over the path they had come. "Those trees—"

"What about them?" he asked absently.

"The way that they grew! Her voice was more animated. "Look, even with those that have fallen, you can see it! That was no grove! They were planted—in lines!"

He followed her pointing finger, studied the logs, the few trunks still standing. Loyse was right, they were not scattered. When they had been rooted firmly they had stood in two parallel lines—marking some long lost roadway? Simon's interest was more than casual, for that way ended at the islet where they rested.

"A road, Simon? An old road? But a road has to lead somewhere!" Loyse got up, faced away from the trees at the island.

It was little enough to cling to, he knew. But any clue which might be a signpost in this unwholesome bog was worth following. A few moments later in a line from the trees Simon came upon evidence to back their guess. The coarse grass was patchy, rooted only here and there, leaving bare expanses of stone. And that stone was smoothed blocks, laid with a care for the joining of one to the next—a pavement. Loyse stamped upon it with the heel of her boot and laughed.

"The road is here! And it will take us out—you shall see, Simon!"

But a road has two ends, Simon thought, and if we have chosen to go the wrong way this could be only leading us deeper into Tormarsh, to confront what or whom dwells there.

It did not take them long to cross the ridge of higher ground, come once more to where water spilled across a dip. But on the other side of that flood stood a tall stone pillar, a little aslant as if the boggy ground had yielded to its weight. On top of that was a ragged tangle of vine, the loops of which drooped in reptilian coils about a carven face.

The beaked nose, the sharply pointed chin, small, overshadowed by that stronger thrust above it, the whole unhuman aspect—

"Volt!" So had that mummy figure they had chanced upon in the sealed cliff cavern appeared in those few minutes before Koris made his plea and took from its dried claws of hands the great ax. What had the seneschal said then? That Volt was a legend—half-god, half-devil —the last of his dead race, living on into the time of human man, giving some of his knowledge to the new-comers because of his loneliness and his compassion. Yet here had once been those who had known Volt well enough to raise a representation of him along some high-way of their kind.

Loyse smiled at the pillar. "You have seen Volt. Koris has told me of that meeting when he begged of the Old One his ax and was not denied. There is none of the Old One lingering here, but I take his stone as a good omen, not one of ill. And he shows us that the road runs on."

There was still that stretch of water ahead. Simon searched the bank of the island and found a length of branch. Stripping away its rotten parts for a core tough enough to serve his purpose, he began to sound that waterway. Some inches of ooze and then solid stone, the pavement ran on. But he did not hurry, feeling for each step before he took it, having Loyse follow directly behind him.

Below the pillar bearing Volt's head the pavement emerged on the higher land once more, and as they went, that strip of solid surface grew wider, until Simon suspected that this was no small islet but a sizable stretch of solid ground. Which would provide living space, and so they could not fear discovery by the Tormen.

"Others have lived here." None of the vegetation grew

tall and Loyse pointed out the blocks of stone which vaguely outlined what had once been walls, stretching away from the road into spike-branched brush. One building? A town or even the remains of a small city? What pleased Simon most was the density of the growth about those blocks. He did not believe that any living thing, save a very small reptile or animal, could force a path through it. And here, on the relative open of the ancient road, he could see any attacker.

The road, which hitherto ran straight, took a curve to the right and Simon caught at Loyse to bring her to an abrupt halt. Those blocks of stone, which had elsewhere tumbled into the negation of any structure, had here been moved, aligned into a low wall. And beyond that wall grew plants in rows, the tending of watchful cultivation plain to read in the weedless soil, the staking of taller stems.

It seemed that here the sunlight, pale and greenish within the swamp world, focused brighter on the plants where buds and blossoms showed as patches of red-purple, while winged insects were busy about that flowering.

"Loquths," Loyse identified the crop, naming a plant which was the mainstay of Estcarp weavers. Those purple flowers would become in due time bolls filled with silken fibers to be picked and spun.

"And look!" She took a step closer to the wall, indicating a small hollow niche constructed of four stones. In that shelter stood a crudely-shaped figure, but there was no mistaking the beaked nose. Whoever had planted that field had left Volt to protect it.

But Simon had sighted something more—a well-trod path, which was not a part of the old road, but ran away from it to the right, winding out of sight on the other side of the field wall.

"Come away!" He was sure that they had made the wrong choice, that the road had brought them into Tormarsh and not toward its fringe. But could they re-

trace their trail? To return to the vicinity of the flyer
might be going directly into enemy hands.

Loyse had already caught his meaning. "The road
continues—" Her voice was lowered to a half whisper.
And the way ahead did look rough and wild enough to
promise that it was no main thoroughfare for those of
Tor. They could only keep on it.

There were no more fields walled and planted. And
even those scattered blocks of ruins disappeared. Only
the fact that now and then they spotted a bare bit of
pavement told them the road still exised.

But their earlier thirst was now more than discomfort, it was agony in mouth and throat. Simon saw Loyse
waver, put his arm about her shoulders to steady her.
They were both staggering when they reached the road's
end—a stone pier which extended into a hellish nightmare of quaking mud, slime and stench. Loyse gave a
cry and turned her head against Simon as he wrenched
them both back and away from that waiting gulf.

10 *JAELITHE FOUND*

"I can go no farther ..."

Simon kept Loyse on her feet with an effort; her
stumbling had become a weaving he could barely support. The sight of the quagmire beyond the road's end
had sapped all her strength.

He was hardly in better case himself. The need for
water, for food, racked him. And he had kept the girl
on her feet only because he was sure that if they gave
way now they might never be able to go on again.

Being so lightheaded Simon did not see the first of those balls which had plopped to the ancient roadway and burst to release a cloud of floury particles. But the second fell almost at their feet, and he had caution enough left to stagger back from it, dragging Loyse with him.

But they were ringed in, the dusty puffs rising and melting into a thin wall about them. Simon held Loyse against him, his dart gun ready. Only one could not fight a cloud rising sluggishly. And he had no doubt that this was a deliberate attack.

"What—?" Loyse's voice was a hoarse croak.

"I don't know!" Simon returned, but he knew enough not to try to cross the line of the cloud.

So far these flaky particles had not reached towards the two they confined. And they arose straight from the broken balls from which they had issued as if still attached to those sources. They were not so thick that Simon could not see beyond. Sooner or later someone would come to the sprung trap—then would be *his* turn. There was a full clip of the three-inch needle points in his dart gun.

Now the cloud began to move. Not in at them but around, speeding in that circling until Simon could no longer distinguish particles but saw only an opaque milky band.

"Simon, I think they are coming!" Loyse pulled a little away, her hand was on knife hilt.

"So do I."

But they were to be given no chance at defense. There was another dull popping sound. A ball from which the circle would not let them retreat, fell, to break. From this came nothing they could see. Only they wilted, to lay still, their hands falling away from the weapons they never had a chance to use.

Simon was in a box and the air was driven from his lungs. He could not breathe—breathe! His whole body was one aching, fighting desire for breath again. Simon

opened his eyes, choking, gasping in pungent fumes
which arose from a saucer being held by his head. He
jerked away from that torment and found he *could*
breathe now, just as he could see.

A wan and murky light came from irregular clusters
on the walls well above where he lay. Stone walls, and
the damp and chill of them reached him. He looked to
the one who held that saucer. In the pallid light perhaps details of features and clothing were not too clear,
but he saw enough to startle him.

Simon lay on a bed for this other sat on a stool and
so was at eye level. Small, but still large-boned enough
to appear misshapen, too long arms, too short legs. The
head, turned so that the eyes met his. Large, the hair
a fine dark down, not like hair at all. And the features
surprisingly regular, handsome in a forbidding way, as
if the emotions behind them were not quite those of
Simon's kind.

The Torman arose. He was quite young, Simon
thought; there was a lank youthfulness about his gangling
body. He wore the breeches-leggings such as were
common to Estcarp, but above them a mail jerkin made
of palm-sized plates laid scallop fashion one over the
other.

With one more measuring stare at Simon the boy
crossed the room, moving with that feline grace which
Simon had always found at odds with Koris' squat frame.
He called, but Simon heard no real words, only a kind
of beeping such as some swamp amphibian might voice.
Then he completely vanished from Simon's sight.

Although the room had a tendency to swing and
sway Simon sat up, steadying himself with his hands. His
fingers moved across the bed coverings, a fabric fine
and silky to the touch. Save for the bed, the stool on
which the young Torman had sat, the room was empty.
It was low of ceiling, with the massive beam across its
middle forming a deep ridge. The lights were clustered
haphazardly about. Then Simon saw one of them move,

leave a cluster of three and crawl slowly to join a singleton!

Though the stone walls were damp and chill, yet the swamp stench did not hang there. Simon got warily to his feet. The radiance of the crawling lights was dim, but he could see all four walls. And in none was there any opening. Where and how had the Torman left?

He was still bemused over that when, a second or so later, he heard a sound behind. To turn quickly almost made him lose his balance. Another figure stood on the far side of the bed, slighter, less ill-proportioned than the boy, but unmistakably of the same race.

She wore a robe which gleamed with small fiery glints, not from any embroidery or outer decorations, but from strands woven into the cloth itself. The down which had fitted the boy's head in a close cap, reached to her shoulders as a fluffy, springing cloud, caught away from her face and eyes by silver clasps on the temples.

The tray she held she put down on the bed for lack of table. Then only did she look at Simon.

"Eat!" It was an order, not an invitation.

Simon sat down again, pulling the tray to him, but still more interested in the woman than what rested on its surface. The paleness of the light could be deceiving but he thought that she was not young. Though there was no outward signs of age such as might appear among his own kind. It was rather an invisible aura which was hers—maturity, wisdom, and also—authority! Whoever she might be, she was a woman of consequence.

He took both hands to raise the beaker of liquid to his lips. It was without any ornament, that wide-mouthed cup, and he thought it was of wood. But its satiny surface and beautiful polish made it a thing of beauty.

The contents were water, but water in which something had been mixed. This was not ale or wine, but an herb drink. At first the taste was bitter, but then that sharp difference vanished and Simon drank eagerly, relishing it the more with every mouthful he sipped.

On a plate of the same shining, polished wood, were cubes of a solid, cheese-seeming substance. As the drink, they had a wry taste upon the first bite, and grew more savory later. All the time Simon ate the woman stood watching him. Yet there was an aloofness about her; she was doing her duty by feeding one whom she found unacceptable. And Simon began to prickle under that realization.

He finished the last cube and then, his faintness gone, he got to his feet, favored the silent watcher with much the same bow as he would have used to greet one of the Guardians.

"My thanks to you, lady."

She made no move to pick up the tray but came forward, around the end of the bed, so that a large cluster of the crawling lights revealed her more clearly. Then Simon saw that the lights were indeed crawling, breaking up their scattered companies to gather along the beam overhead.

"You are of Estcarp." A statement and yet a question as if, looking upon him, the woman doubted that.

"I serve the Guardians. But I am not of the Old Blood." His appearance, Simon decided, was what puzzled her.

"Of Estcarp." Now it was a statement. "Tell me, witch warrior, who commands in Estcarp—you?"

"No. I am Border Warder of the south. Koris of Gorm is marshal and seneschal."

"Koris of Gorm. And what manner of man is Koris of Gorm?"

"A mighty warrior, a good friend, a keeper of oaths, and one who has been hurt from his birth." From whence had come those words for his use? They were not phrased to match his thinking, yet what he had said was the truth.

"And how came the Lord of Gorm to serve the witches?"

"Because he was never truly lord of Gorm. When his

father died his stepmother called in Kolder to establish the rule for her own son. And Koris, escaping Kolder, came to Estcarp. He wishes not Gorm, for Gorm under Kolder died, and he was never happy there."

"Never happy there— But why was he not happy? Kolder was a kindly man and a good one."

"But those of his following would never let Koris forget he was—strange . . ." Simon hesitated, striving to choose the right words. Koris' mother had come from Tormarsh. This woman could even be kin to the seneschal.

"Yes." She did not add to that but asked a very different question. "This maid who was taken with you, what is she to you?"

"A friend—one who has been with me in battle. And she is betrothed to Koris who seeks her now!" If there was any advantage to be gained from the thread of connection between the seneschal and the marsh people, then Loyse must have it.

"Yet they say she is duchess in Karsten. And there is war between the witches and those of Karsten."

It would seem that Tormarsh, for all its taboo-locked borders, still heard the news from outside the swamp.

"The story is long—"

"There is time," she told him flatly, "for the telling of it. And I would hear."

There was a definite order in that. Simon began, cutting the tale to bare outline, but telling of the ax marriage made for Loyse in Verlaine's towers and all that happened thereafter. But when he spoke of the shipwreck on the coast and how he, Koris, and two survivors of the Guard, had climbed to discover themselves in the long-lost tomb of Volt, where Koris had boldly claimed Volt's ax from the hands of the mummified dead, the Torwoman halted him abruptly, made him go into details. She questioned and requestioned him on small points, such as the words, as well as he could remember, that Koris had used when he asked the ax of Volt,

and how that ax had been taken easily, with the long
dead body crumbling into dust once the shaft had been
withdrawn from the claw hands.

"Volt's ax—he bears Volt's ax!" she said when he was
done. "This must be thought upon."

Simon expelled his breath in a gasp. She was gone—
as if she had never stood there, solid body on solid
pavement. He took two strides to the same spot where
she had been standing only an instant earlier, drove his
boot down in a stamp which proved the footing as solid
as it looked. But—she was gone!

Hallucination? Had she ever been here at all? Or was
this one of those mind-twisting tricks such as the
witches played? Shape-changing—that was as eerie in it-
way as this instant vanishing. So this could be another
form of magic, with its own rules, simple enough when
one was trained by those rules. And not only the Torwoman practiced it, for the boy had winked out in just
the same way. But to those who did not know the trick,
this room or others like it would continue to be prison
cells.

Simon returned to the bed. The tray with its beaker
and plate still rested there. That much was real. And the
fact that his hunger and thirst was gone, that he felt
strong and able again—that was no hallucination.

He had been captured and imprisoned. But he had
also been fed, and so far he had not been threatened.
His dart gun was gone, but he had expected to be dis-
armed. What did these marsh dwellers want? He and
Loyse had come into their territory by accident. He
knew that they resented all trespassing bitterly, but
were they fanatical enough on that subject to hold the
innocent equally guilty with any determined invader?

Did they close their borders to everyone? Simon remembered Aldis, her hands tight upon the Kolder talisman, so deeply sunk in her voiceless call for aid that she
was unaware of action about her. She must have expected such aid—so Kolder crawled somewhere in Tor-

marsh as evilly as the lizard thing had crawled upon the flyer.

Kolder. To those of witch blood Kolder was a void, noticeable in its presence because of that void. In the times past he, too, had known Kolder by sensing it—not as a void but as a waiting menace. Could he pick up the canker now the same way?

Simon set the tray on the stool, stretched himself once more on the bed, closed his eyes, and set his will free. He had always had this gift of foreseeing, in part a limping gift, not to be disciplined into any real service. But he was sure that since he had come to Estcarp that gift had grown, strengthened. Jaelithe—the twist of pain which always came now with the thought of Jaelithe. She had used the symbols of power between them twice and those had glowed in answer. So that she had hailed him as one of her kind, then . . .

Now, though he intended to go hunting for the cancer of Kolder, rather did his mind return again and again to Jaelithe, to pictures of her. First, as he had seen her fleeing in rags with the hounds of Alizon baying on her trail, then as she had ridden in mail and war helm to Sulcarkeep when Kolder had made its first foul move in the present war. Jaelithe, kneeling on the quay of that fortress, breathing witchery into the scraps of sail for the vessels they had hastily whittled from wood, tossing those crude ships into the sea, so that a mighty fleet moved out through the cloaking mist to confound the enemy. Jaelithe acting as a sorceress and reader of fortunes, brewer of love potions in Kars, when her summoning had brought him across many miles to her aid. Jaelithe, shape-changed into a hideous hag and riding in company over the border to rouse Estcarp for war. Jaelithe in Gorm, telling him in her own way that that way was also his from then on. Jaelithe in his arms, being one with him in a way no other woman had ever been before, or would ever be again. Jaelithe excited, bright-eyed, that last morning, in the belief that her witchcraft had not gone from her at all, but that she was all she had been. Jaelithe—gone from him as if she used the traveling magic of these Torfolk.

Jaelithe! Simon did not cry that aloud, but inside of him it was one great shout of longing. Jaelithe!

"Simon!"

His eyes snapped open, he was staring up into the gloom, for the crawling lights had returned to their scattered clusters along the walls.

No, that had not come in any audible voice. Breathing fast, he closed his eyes again. "Jaelithe?"

"Simon." Firm, assured, as she had ever been.

"You are here?" He thought that, trying to shape the words clearly in his mind as a man might fumble about in a foreign tongue of which he knew little.

"No—in body—no."

"You *are* here!" he replied with a conviction he could not explain.

"In a way, Simon—because you are—I am. Tell me, Simon, where *are* you?"

"Somewhere within Tormarsh."

"So much is already known, since we are aware that your flyer dropped there. But, you are no longer Kolder ruled."

"Fulk's belt—one of the bosses on it—their planting."

"Yes, it opened a gate for them. But you were never so much theirs that we could not alter their spell a little. That is why you did not fly seaward at their bidding, but inland. Tormarsh is no ally of ours, but perhaps there is better chance to treat with Tormarsh than Kolder."

"Kolder is here also." Simon told her what he believed to be the truth. "Aldis called their aid, she was calling when we left her."

"Ah!"

"Jaelithe!" That moment of withdrawal frightened him.

"I hear. But if Kolder is with you—"

"I was trying to search for it."

"So? Well, perhaps in that two may be better than

one, my dear lord. Think you on Aldis. If she moved to Kolder, perhaps your power may move with her—to our better knowledge."

Simon tried to picture Aldis as he had seen her last, lying in the flyer as he pushed back the sprung door. But he discovered that he could not visualize that clearly at all. Instead he had momentary flashes of quite another and nonfamiliar scene—of Aldis seated, leaning forward, speaking eagerly to—to a blankness. And upon that the tie, if tie it was, with Aldis snapped.

"Kolder!" Jaelithe's recognition was sharp as any blow. "And they are on the move, I think. Listen well, Simon. The Guardians say that my power is now only a wisp which will fail with the passing of time, that I have no place now in the Council of Es. But I tell you that between us we have something that I do not understand, for it is different than all else which I have held in my witchhood. Therefore, though it has taken me time to test this thing, to work with it as best I can, I have learned that I am not able to shape or aim it, save with you. Perhaps both of us must be the united vessel for this new strength. Sometimes it rages within me until I fear that I cannot hold it in bonds. But we have so little time to learn it. Kolder is on the move and it may be that we cannot bring you forth from Tormarsh before that move is made—"

"I do not wear their talisman, but it may be that they can control me still," he warned her. "If so, can they reach you through me?"

"I do not know. I have learned so little! It is like trying to shape fire with my two hands! But this we can do—"

Again a snapping—even more sharp than that break which had come between him and the shadow shape of Aldis.

"Jaelithe!" he shouted soundlessly. But this time—no reply.

II *KOLDER KIND*

SIMON LAY very still, sweating now. For this was no half-trance of his own willing. He was motionless in bonds he could not see, his body held by another's will. Then she stood there, clear to the sight, at the foot of the bed, watching him in the level measurement which held no hint of whether she was friend or foe, or merely neutral in this war.

"They have come," she said, "to answer the call of their woman they have come."

"Kolder!" Simon found that he could use his tongue and lips if not the rest of his body.

"The dead ones who serve such," the Torwoman qualified. "Listen, man who obeys Estcarp, we have no quarrel with the witches. Between them and us there is neither friendship nor enmity. We were here when the Old Race came and built Es and their other dark towers. We have been rooted here for long and long, a handful of people who can remember when man was not the ruler of earthside, not even ones who lived widely. We are of those Volt gathered and set apart to learn his wisdom.

"And we want no dealings with those outside Tormarsh. You have come to trouble us with your wars which are no concern of ours. The swifter you are gone from us, the better served we shall be."

"But if you do not favor the witches, then why do you favor Kolder? Kolder hungers for rule over all men—and that includes the race of Tor," Simon retorted.

"We do not favor Kolder, we only ask that we be

left to our own mysteries without troubling from beyond the marsh rim. The witches have not threatened us. This you call Kolder has shown us what will happen if we do not yield you to them now. And so it is decided that you go—"

"But Estcarp would defend you against Kolder—" Simon began until she smiled a small, cold smile.

"Will they, with aught save good wishes, Warder of the Border? There is no war between us, but they fear the marsh as a place of ancient mysteries and strange ways. Would they fight to save it? I think not. Also they have no men to throw into such a battle now."

"Why?" She seemed so certain that Simon was startled into a rough demand.

"Alizon has risen. Estcarp needs must throw all her armies northward to hold the marches there. No, we make the best bargain for us."

"And so I am to be delivered to the Kolder." Simon strove to keep his voice even and emotionless. "And what of Loyse? Do you give her also into the hands of the worst enemy this world has ever known?"

"The worst?" the Torwoman echoed. "Ah, we have seen many nations rise and fall, and in each generation there is a powerful enemy to be faced, either with victory or defeat. As for the girl—she is part of the bargain."

"She is also Koris', and I think you will discover that that has a meaning when it comes to extracting a price for such bargaining. I have seen the price he took from Verlaine and from Kars. Volt's gift drank deep in both those holds. Your marshland will not turn him back when it comes to his hunting."

"The bargain is made," her tone was more remote than ever. Then her hands came up in a swift gesture and her fingers moved. Not to shape Jaelithe's symbol of power, but still in an air-borne sketch which had meaning.

"So you deem this Koris will come hunting for vengeance here?" she asked. "This pale-faced girl means so much to him?"

"She does, and those who have harmed her have need to fear."

"Ah, but now he must ride to hold back Alizon. It will be many days before he shall have time to think of aught else. Or perhaps he will find an end to all questions and desires among the border hillocks."

"And I say to you, lady, that Volt's gift shall yet swing in Tormarsh if you do as you have said."

"If *I* do, March Lord? I have naught to say in the yea and nay of such bargainings."

"No?" Simon put all the skepticism he could muster into that. "And I say that you are not the least of those among the Tor born."

She did not answer for a long moment, her gaze steady upon him.

"Perhaps once I was not. Now I do not raise my voice in any council. I wish you no ill, Warder of Estcarp. And I think that you mean no ill to me—or any of us. But when need drives, we obey. This much I shall do for you, since the maid is favored by he who was once lord of Gorm. I shall send a message forth to Es that those there may know where you have gone and why. If then they can move to aid you, perhaps it will not go so ill. More than that I am sworn not to do."

"The Kolder come for us here—how?" Simon demanded.

"They come—or at least their servants come—up the inner river in one of their ships."

"But there *is* no river linking Tormarsh with the sea!"

"No outer one," she agreed. "The marsh drains under ground. They have found that way to us, they have already visited us by it before."

By submarine down an underground river, Simon faced that. Even if the promised message reached Es in time to send a small force to the rescue, they could not ferret out the enemies' pathway, or help the prisoners borne so along it. The Guard of Estcarp would not be the answer.

"If you would truly favor us to the point of sending any message," Simon told her, "then send it not to Es but to the Lady Jaelithe."

"If she is your wife, then she is no witch, nor can she do aught to aid you." The Torwoman stared at him again with a curiosity which Simon thought dangerous.

"Nevertheless, if you favor us in so much—then send."

"I have said that I will send, if you wish it. To the Lady Jaelithe it shall be. Now, they come to take you hence, March Lord. If you survive this captivity, remember that Tormarsh is old, there is that within it which has stood long without being stamped into the bog with those who know its ways. Do not think that what is here can be easily swept aside."

"Say that rather to Volt's gift and he who bears it, lady. From Kolder's fingers few escape. But Koris lives, and rides, and hates—"

"Let him ride and hate and show Volt's gift to Alizon. There is the need for action there. Odd, March Warder, there is that in you which does not align itself with your words. You speak as one who resigns himself to fate, yet I do not believe that is so. Now—" Once again she sketched a sign in the air. "The gate is open and it is time you go."

What happened then was beyond any description Simon was ever able to give. He only knew that one moment he was in the doorless cell, and the next, still helpless in whatever hold they had upon him, he was in the open on the bank of a dark lake where the water was thick and murky, with a threatening look to it.

There was the murmur of voices about and behind him, the Torfolk were gathered there, men and women. And a little apart the smaller group of which Simon was an unwilling part.

Aldis, a look of confidence and expectancy on her

face, Loyse, standing so stiffly that Simon guessed she was held in the same immobile spell as himself, and two of the Tormen. There was also a fifth from beyond the marsh boundaries.

No Kolder—at least not the Kolder such as he had seen in Gorm. Of middle size, face round and dark of skin, a kind of tan-yellow unlike any Simon had seen in this world, though they had found representatives of unknown races among the dead slaves in Gorm. He wore a tight-fitting one-piece garment of gray, like the Kolder dress, but his head was bare of any cap though he had a silvery disk resting under the fringe of his thin, reddish hair at the temple.

And the stranger was weaponless. However on the breast of his suit there was one of those intertwined knots fashioned of green metal, such as had been on Fulk's swordbelt and Aldis carried.

The murmur from the Tormen grew louder, so that individual beepings carried to Simon. For the first time he wondered, with a small surge of hope, if the bargain the woman had told him about, had been so widely accepted as she would have him believe. Could an appeal from him now split the ranks, give the prisoners a chance? But, even as Simon thought that, one of the marsh natives, standing with Aldis, raised his arm in a lashing motion. There was a ring of bells, the first really melodious sound Simon had heard in this half-drowned country. As the chain bearing those fell again to the Torman's side there was quiet, instant and absolute.

Quiet enough so that the disturbance in the murky water of the lake broke in an audible bubble on the surface. Then the water poured away as out of the depths arose the mud-streaked surface of a Kolder underwater vessel. There were scars and scrapes along its sides as if it had found whatever passage ran this way a difficult one. It moved without sound closer to shore.

An opening in the rounded upper surface flipped to shore to form a platform bridge uniting land and ship.

Aldis, her eager expression now an open smile, started along that pathway. Then Loyse, as if Aldis pulled her by cords, followed, walking stiffly, her whole body expressing her fear and repulsion. Simon's turn—his muscles, his bones, his flesh, were no longer his own. Only his mind imprisoned in that helpless body struggled for freedom, with defeat for the end.

He walked to that opening in the Kolder ship. Then, still by another's will, his hands and feet found holds on a ladder, and he descended into the space below. But not to freedom. Loyse moved ahead and he after, into a small cabin bare of any furnishings. They stood, he slightly behind the girl, and heard the door clang shut. Then and then only, did the compulsion cease to hold him.

Loyse, with a little moan, slumped and Simon caught her. He lowered her gently to the metal flooring but still held her as their bodies tingled with the vibration reaching them through the structure of the ship. Whatever power moved the submarine was now in force; the voyage had begun.

"Simon," Loyse's head turned so that he felt her breath come in gasps, not far from sobs, against his cheek. "Where are they taking us?"

This was a time when only the truth would serve. "To where we have wished to be—though not under these circumstances—I think, the Kolder base."

"But—" her voice quavered to a pause. When she spoke again it was with a measure of self-control, "that—that lies overseas."

"And we travel under water." Simon leaned back against the wall. As far as he could see the cabin was bare and they had no weapons. Not only that, but there was that control over them the Kolder appeared able to use at will, leaving all hopes of rebellion doomed. But, perhaps there was one way . . .

"They will never know where we are. Koris cannot—" Loyse was traveling her own path of thought.

"At present Koris is occupied, they have seen to that also." Simon told her of the invasion from Alizon. "They plan to bay Estcarp around with snarling dogs, letting her wear down her forces with such blows, none of which will yet be fatal, but which will exhaust her manpower and her resources—"

"Letting others do their fighting," Loyse broke in hotly, "ever the Kolder way."

"But one which can win for them as time passes," Simon commented. "They have some plan for us also."

"What?"

"By right of marriage you are now Duchess of Karsten, and so a piece worth controlling in this devious game they play. I am Border Warder. They can use me as hostage or—" He hated to put into words the other reason which might make him valuable to the enemy, the much more logical one.

"Or they can strive to make you one of them and so a traitor to serve their ends among the ranks of Estcarp!" Loyse stated it for him. "But there is one thing we may do so that we cannot be used so. We can die." Her eyes were very somber.

"If the need comes," Simon replied crisply. He was thinking: the site of the Kolder base—that was what they had long wanted to know. Not to snap off the monster's hands and arms, but destroy the head. Only, the world was wide and Estcarp had no clues as to the direction in which such a base lay. The Kolder use of underwater ships meant that they could not successfully be tracked by the Sulcarmen who counted the ocean their true home.

But suppose that Kolder *could* be tracked? The Sulcarmen were not truly land fighters. Certainly their raiders would be now harrying the coast of Alizon with the hit and run tactics they had developed to a high art, but that employment would not require the majority of their fleet. And if that fleet were free to track a Kolder ship, find their base—their fighting crews would harass the enemy on their home ground until Estcarp could throw the might of striking power against that hold.

"You have a plan?" The fear which had shadowed Loyse's features was fading as she watched Simon.

"Not quite a plan," he said. "Just a small hope. But—"

It was that "but" which was all important now. The Kolder ship would have to be traced. *Could* that be done by contact such as he and Jaelithe had had in the Tormarsh village? Would the blight of those barriers the Kolder had always been able to use to cloak themselves against the magic of Estcarp sunder them utterly? So many "ifs" and "buts" and only his scrap of hope to answer all of them.

"Listen—" More to clear his own thinking than because he expected any active assistance from Loyse, Simon outlined what that hope might be. She gripped his arm fiercely.

"Try it! Try to reach Jaelithe now! Before they take us so far away that even thought can not span that journey. Try it now!"

In that she could be right. Simon closed his eyes, put his head back against the wall and once more bent his whole desire and will-to-touch on Jaelithe. He had no guide in this seeking, no idea of how it might be done, he had only the will which he used with every scrap of energy he could summon.

"I hear—"

Simon's heart beat with a heavier thump at that reply.

"We go . . . on Kolder ship . . . perhaps to their base. Can you follow?"

There was no immediate answer, but neither was that snap of breaking contact which he had known twice before. Then came her reply.

"I do not know, but if it is possible, it shall be done!"

Again silence, but abiding with Simon the sense of union. His concentration was broken, not by his will, nor Jaelithe's, but by a sudden lurch of the ship, sending his body skidding along the cabin wall, Loyse on top of him. The vibration through those walls was stepped up until the vessel quivered.

"What is it?" Loyse's voice was thin and ragged once again.

The flooring was aslant so that the sub could not be on an even keel. And the vibration had become an actual shaking of its fabric and frame as if it were engaged in some struggle. Simon remembered the scars and mud smudges he had seen on its sides. An underground passage by river might not be too accommodating. They could have nosed into a bank, caught there. He said so.

Loyse's hands twisted together. "Can they get us loose?"

Simon saw the wide blankness of her eyes, caught the claustrophobic panic rising in her.

"I would say that whoever captains this vessel would know how to deal with such problems; this is not the first time—by Tormarsh accounts—that they have made the run." But there was always a first time for disaster. Simon had never believed that he would reach the point of joining the Kolder in any wish, but now he did as he tensed at every movement of the ship. They must be backing water to pull loose. The cabin rocked about the two prisoners, spilling them back and forth across its slick floor.

The rocking stopped and then the ship gave a great jerk. Once more the vibration sank to an even purr, they must be free and on course once again.

"I wonder how far we are from the sea?"

Simon had thought about that, too. He did not know where Jaelithe was, how long it would take her to contact any Sulcar ship and send it skulking after them. But Jaelithe would be on that ship—she would have to sail thus in order to hold the tie with him! And they could not assemble a fleet so quickly. Suppose that single Sulcar vessel lurking behind would be sighted, or otherwise detected by the Kolder? An engagement would be no contest at all, the Sulcar ship, and its crew would be helpless before the weapons of the Kolder. It was rank folly for him to encourage Jaelithe to follow. He must not try to reach her again—let her believe that he could not—

Jaelithe—Kolder. They balanced in his mind. How could he have been so insane as to draw her into such a plan?

"Because it is not rank folly, Simon! We do not yet know the limits of this we hold, what we dare summon by it—"

This time he had not tried to reach her, yet she had read all his forebodings as if he had hurled them at her.

"Remember, I follow! Find this noisome nest—and there shall be a clearing of it!"

Confidence. She was riding high on a way of confidence. But Simon could not match that, he could only see every pointed reef ahead and no discernible course among them.

12   SHE WHO WILL NOT WAIT

THE ROOM was low and long, dark save where the shutters were well open to the call of the sea, the light which came over those restless waves. And the woman who sat by the table was as turbulent within as those waves, though she showed little outward sign of her concern. She wore leather and mail; the chain-mail scarfed helm, winged like that of any Borderer, sat on the table board to her right hand. And at her left was a tall cage in which perched a white falcon as silent and yet as aware as she. Between her fingers a small roll of bark rolled back and forth.

One of the witches? The captain of the Sulcar cruiser was still trying to assess her as he came from the door to front her. He had been summoned from the dockside to this tavern by one of the Borderers, for what reason he could not guess.

But when the woman looked at him, he thought that this was no witch. He did not see her gem of power. Only, neither was she any common dame. He sketched a half salute as he would have to any of his fellow captains.

"I am Koityi Stymir, at your summoning, Wise One." Deliberately he used the witch address to see her reaction.

"And I am Jaelithe Tregarth," she replied without amplification. "They tell me, Captain, that you are about to put to sea on patrol—"

"Raiding," he corrected her, "up Alizon way."

The falcon shifted on its cage perch, its very bright eyes on the man. He had an odd feeling that it was as intelligently interested in his answer as the woman.

"Raiding," she repeated. "I come to offer you something other than a raid, Captain. Although it may not put loot into your empty hold and it may bring you far greater danger than any Alizon sword or dart you may face in the north."

Jaelithe studied the seafarer. As all his race he was tall, wide of shoulder, fair of hair. Young as he was, there was a self-confidence in his carriage which spoke of past success and a belief in the future. She had not had time to choose widely, but what she had heard of Stymir along the waterfront made her send for him out of all the captains now in port at the mouth of the River Es.

There was this about the Sulcar breed: adventure and daring had a pull on them, sometimes over that of certain gain in trade, loot in war. It was that strain in their character which made them explorers as well as merchant traders in far seas. And she must depend upon that quality now to attract Stymir to her service.

"And what do you have to offer me, lady?"

"A chance to find the Kolder base," she told him boldly. This was no time to fence. Time—that inner turmoil boiled in her until she could hardly control it—time was her slave driver in this venture.

For a long moment he stared at her and then he spoke: "For years have we sought that, lady. How comes it now into your hands that you can speak so, as if you held a map to it?"

"I have no map, but still a method to find it—or believe that this is possible. But time grows short, and this depends upon time." And distance? her mind questioned. Could Simon get beyond the reach of their tie and she lose contact with him?

She twisted the roll of bark which had come out of Tormarsh, which had been an argument with the Guardians.

Her inner conflict might have been communicated to the great falcon, for now it mantled and screamed, even as it might scream in battle.

"You believe in what you say, lady," Stymir conceded. "The Kolder base—" With his finger tip he traced a design on the table board between them. "The Kolder base!"

But when he raised his eyes again to meet hers there was a wariness in them.

"There are tales among us—that the Kolder have a way of distorting minds and so sending those who were once our friends, even our cup-comrades, to lead us into their traps."

Jaelithe nodded. "That is indeed the truth, Captain, and you do well to think about such a risk. But, I am of the Old Race, and I have been a witch. You know that the Kolder taint cannot touch any of my kind."

"Have been a witch—" He caught and held to that.

"And why am I not one now?" She brought herself to answer that, though the need for doing so rasped her raw. "Because I am now wife to him whc is March Warder of Estcarp. Have you not heard of the outlander who helped lead the storming of Sippar—Simon Tregarth?"

"Him!" There was wonder in the captain now. "Aye, we have heard of him. Then you, lady, rode to Sulcarkeep for its last battle. Aye, you have met Kolder and you know Kolder! Tell me what you now devise."

Jaelithe began her tale, the one she had set in mind before this meeting. When she had done the captain's amazement was marked.

"And you think this we can do, lady?"

"I go myself to its doing."

"To find the Kolder base—to lead in a fleet upon the finding. Aye, such a feat as that the bards would sing for a hundred hundred years to come! This is a mighty business, lady. But where is the fleet?"

"The fleet follows, but only one ship may lead. We do not know what devices these Kolder have in their below-water ship, how well they may be able to track anything on the surface. One ship above, not too close —that they might not suspect. A fleet could have but one meaning for them, and then, would they knowingly lead us to their den?"

Captain Stymir nodded. "Clearly thought, my lady. So then how do we bring in the fleet?"

Jaelithe lifted her hand to the cage. "Thus. This one has been trained by the Falconers to return whence it came, bearing any message. I have already conferred with those in authority. The fleet will assemble, cruise out to sea. When the message comes, why—then they will move in. But this is a matter of time. If the under-seas' ship issues from the marsh river and has too great a lead, then I am not sure we can contact my lord, captive in it."

"This river, draining from Tormarsh . . ." It was plain that the captain was trying to align points along the shore to make a picture he knew. "I would guess it to be the Enkere—to the north. We could pose as a raider on the course to Alizon and so reach that spot without raising any undue interest."

"And may we sail soon?"

"Now if you wish, lady. The supplies are aboard, the crew gathered. We were off to Alizon today."

"This voyage may be longer; your supplies for coast raiding are limited."

"True. But there is the *Sword Bride* in from the south; she carries supplies for the army. We may transship from her if you have the authority. And that will take but a small measure of time."

"I have the authority. Let us be about it!"

The Guardians might not believe that she would retain this power of hers, but they had granted her backing for now. Jaelithe frowned. To have to use one of the Seakeep witches to transmit that request and her message had been galling, but she was willing to face any rebuff to gain her ends. And she had proved, when she had used the falcon and her new perception to confuse Simon in the flyer, that she did have something they could not dismiss as useless. Kolder would only die when its heart was blasted. And if she and Simon, working together, could find that heart, then all witchdom would back them to the limit.

Captain Stymir was as good as his boast. It still lacked several hours of nightfall when his *Wave Cleaver* skimmed out of the harbor, heading towards the black blot of Gorm and so beyond for the open sea. She had chosen better than she knew, Jaelithe decided, when she had picked Stymir from the four captains in the harbor. His ship was small, but she was swift, a cruiser rather than one of the wider-bottomed merchant carriers.

"You have been an opener of ways, Captain?" she asked as they stood together by the great rudder sweep.

"Aye, lady. It was my thought to try for the far north—had this war with Kolder not broken on our heads. There is a village I have visited—odd people, small, dark, with a click-click speech of their own we cannot rightly twist tongue around. But they offer such furs as I have seen nowhere else—only a few of them. Silver those furs, long of hair, but very soft. When we asked whence they came, this click-click speech folk said that they are brought once a year by a caravan of wild men from the north. They have other wares, too. Look you—"

He slipped from his wrist a band of metal and offered it to her. Jaelithe turned the ring about in her fingers. Gold, but a paler gold than she had ever seen before. Old, very old, and there was a design, so worn that it was merely curves and hollows. Yet there was sophistication, a degree of art in that worn design which did not say primitive but hinted of civilization—only what civilization?

"This I traded for two years ago in that village, and all they could tell me was that it came from the north with the wild men. Look you, here and here." He touched with finger tip two points on the band, "That is a star—very much worn away and yet a star. And on the very, very old things of my people there are some-times such stars—"

"Another trader of your people ages ago who made a voyage there and returned not?"

"Perhaps. But there is also another thought. For we have bard songs, also very old, of whence we first came —and that there was cold, and snow, and much battling with monsters of the dark."

Jaelithe thought of how Simon had come to Estcarp,

and of that gate in another place through which the Kolder had issued to trouble them. These Sulcarmen, always restless, ever at sea, taking their families with them on such voyages as if they might not return. Only in the times of outright war were Sulcar ships other than floating villages. Had they, too, come through a gate which kept them searching with some hidden instinct to find again? She gave the band back to Stymir.

"A quest of value, Captain. May there be long years for each of us for the questing we hold in our hearts."

"Well spoken, lady. Now we are approaching the mouth of the Enkere. Do you wish to hunt in your own way for the Kolder water sulker?"

"I do."

She lay on the bunk in the small cabin to which the captain had shown her. It was hot and close and the mail shirt constricted her breathing. But Jaelithe strove to set aside all outward things, to build in her mind the picture of Simon. There were many Simons and all had depth of meaning for her, but it was necessary to forge those into one upon which to center her call.

But—no answer . . . She had been so sure of instant contact that that silence was like an unexpected blow. Jaelithe opened her eyes and gazed up at the roofing of the ship's timbers so close above her head. The *Wave Cleaver* was truly cleaving waves and the motion about her—perhaps that was what broke the contact or kept her from completing it.

"Simon!" Her call searched, demanded. She had had long years of training as a witch, to center and aim her power through that jewel which was the badge of her office. Was this fumbling now because she must do it all without a tool, with the skepticism of those she had long revered eating at her confidence?

She had been so sure that morning when she had had that sending concerning Loyse and when she had ridden to Es with that flaming desire to be one of the Power again—only to find doors and minds closed against all her knocking. Then, because she had been so sure she was right, she had gone apart, as dictacted by her past training, to study this thing, to strive to use it. And when she had had the tidings that Simon had acted against all nature, she had guessed that the Kolder blight had touched him, then she had used that new power, little as she knew about it, in the fight for Simon which dropped him into the forbidden tangle of Tormarsh. After that, she had tried again with purpose. But were the Guardians right, was this new thing she thought she had found merely the dying echo of the old power, doomed to fail?

Simon. Jaelithe began to consider Simon apart from a goal at which to aim thought. And from the fringe consideration of Simon she looked inward at herself. She had surrendered her witchdom to Simon when she wedded him, thinking this union meant more to her than all else, accepting the penalty for that uniting. But why then had she been so eager to seize upon this hope that her sacrifice had been no sacrifice at all? She had left Simon to ride to Es, to best the Guardians and prove that she was not as others, that she was still witch as well as wife. And when they would not believe, she had not sought out Simon, she had kept to herself, intent upon proving them wrong. As if—as if Simon was no longer of importance at all! Always the power—the power!

Was that because she had known no other force in her life? That what Simon had awakened in her was not lasting emotion, but merely a new thing which had been strange and compelling enough to shake her from the calm and ordered ways of her kind, but not deep enough to hold her? Simon—

Fear—fear that such reasoning was forcing her to face something harsh and unbearable. Jaelithe concentrated again on Simon: standing so, with his head held high, his grave face so seldom alight with any smile—and yet in his eyes, always in his eyes when they met hers—

Jaelithe's head turned on the hard pillow of the bunk. Simon—or the need to know that she was still a witch. Which drove her now? As a witch she had never known this kind of fear—not without—but within.

"Simon!" That was not a demanding summons for communication; it was a cry born of pain and self-doubt.

"Jaelithe . . ." Faint, far off, but yet an answer, and in it something which steadied her, though it did not answer her questions.

"We come." She added as tersely as she could what she had done to further his plan for tracking.

"I do not know where we are," he made answer. "And I can hardly reach you."

That was the danger: that their bond might fail. If they only had some way of strengthening that. In shape-changing one employed the common linkage of mutual desire to accomplish that end. Mutual desire—but they were only two. Two—no. Loyse—Loyse's desire would link with theirs in this. But how? The girl from Ver-laine had no vestige of witch power. She had been unable to perform the simplest spells in spite of Jae-lithe's coaching, having the blindness in that direction which enfeebled all but the Old Race.

But shape-changing worked on those who were not of the Old Race; it had once worked on Loyse in Kars. She might not be able to pull on the power itself, but it could react upon her. And was this still *the* power?

Without answering Simon Jaelithe broke the faint link between them, set in her mind instead the image of Loyse as she had last seen the girl weeks ago in Es and using that as anchorage she sought the spirit behind the picture.

Loyse!

Jaelithe had a blurred, momentary glimpse of a wall, a scrap of floor, and another crouching figure that was

Simon! Loyse—for that single instant she had looked through Loyse's eyes!

But possession was not what she wanted, contact rather. Again she tried. This time with a message, not so deep an identification. Foggy, as if that wisp of tie between them fluttered, anchored for an instant, and then failed. But as Jaelithe struggled to make it firm, it did unite and become less tenuous. Until it held Loyse. Now for Simon—

Groping, anchorage! Simon, Loyse—and it *was* stronger, more consistent. Also—she gained direction from it! What they had wanted from the first—direction!

Jaelithe wriggled from the confines of the bunk, kept her footing with the aid of handgrips as she sought the deck. There was wind billowing the sails, the narrow knife of the bow dipped into rising waves. The sky was sullen where the sun had gone, leaving only a few richly colored banners at the horizon.

That wind whipped Jaelithe's hair about her uncovered head, sent spray into her face until she gasped as she reached the post beside the rudder where two of the crew labored to hold the ship on course, and Captain Stymir watched narrowly sky, wind and wave.

"The course," Jaelithe caught at his shoulder to steady herself at an unexpected incline of the decking. "That way—"

It was so sharp set in her head that she could pivot in a half turn and point, sure that her bearings were correct for their purpose. He studied her for a second as if to gauge her sincerity and then nodded, taking the helm himself.

The bow of the *Wave Cleaver* began to swing to Jaelithe's left, coming about with due caution for wind and wave, away from the dark shadow of the land, out into the sea. Somewhere under the surface of all this turbulence was that other vessel, and Jaelithe had no doubts at all that they were going to follow the track of that, as long as that three-fold awareness linked Simon, Loyse and herself.

She stood now wet with spray, her hair lankly plastered to her skull, stringing on her shoulders. The last colors faded from the sky or were blotted out by the cloud masses. Behind them even the shadow of Estcarp's coast had gone. She knew so little of the sea. This fury of wind and wave spelled storm, and could storm so batter them from the course that they would lose the quarry?

Jaelithe shouted that question to the captain.

"A blow—" His words came faintly back. "But we have ridden out far worse and still kept on course. What can be done, will be. For the rest, lady, it lies between the fingers of the Old Woman!" He spat over his shoulder in the ritual luck-evoking gesture of his race.

But still she would not go below, watching in the fast gathering darkness for something she knew she would not be able to see with the eyes of her body, making as best she could an anchor past breaking for the tie.

13 KOLDER NEST

TIME WAS hard to measure in this ship's cell. Simon lay relaxed on a narrow shelf bunk, but still he held to that ribbon of communication which included not only Jaelithe, but now Loyse in a lesser degree. Though the girl no longer shared his quarters, she was present in his mind.

Simon had seen none of his captors since, shortly

after this voyage had begun, Aldis appeared and took charge of Loyse, leaving him alone. A second inspection of the narrow cabin had provided some amenities: a bunk which could be pulled out and down from the wall, a sliding shelf on which, from time to time, a tray of food appeared—coming from the wall behind.

The food was emergency rations, he thought, thin wafers without much taste, a small can of liquid. Not appetizing but enough to keep hunger and thirst under control. Otherwise there was no break in the long, silent hours. He did sleep a little while Loyse took over, holding the tie. Simon gathered that she now shared Aldis' cabin, but that the Kolder agent was leaving her alone, content that she was passive.

Seven, now eight mealtimes. Simon counted them off. But that gave him no reasonable idea of the number of hours or days he had been here under the unchanging glow of the walls. They could be feeding him twice daily, or even once; he could not be sure. This was a period of waiting, and to any man who had depended most of his life upon the stimulation of action, waiting was a harsh ordeal. Only once before had it been so—during a year in jail. Waiting then, warped by the bitterness of knowing that he had been duped into taking punishment for those he hated, he had spent that time striving to work out schemes for repayment.

Now he was facing a blind future without even a good knowledge of the nature of the enemy. All he had was that mental picture from the past of the Kolder leader dying in Gorm, a narrow valley down which strange vehicles dashed while those in them fired back at pursuers. There had been another world for the Kolders and something had gone wrong there.

Somehow they had discovered a "gate" and come through—into this time and place, where the civilization of the Estcarpian Old Race was on the wane, a slow slip into the age-old dust which already rose about

Es and the villages and cities of their kind. Along the coast—in Alizon and Karsten—a more barbaric upswing was rooted, newer nations, elbowing aside the Old Race, yet so much in awe of their legendary witches that they dared not quite challenge them—not until the Kolder began to meddle.

And if Kolder was not uprooted, Alizon and Karsten would go the way of Gorm: ingested into the horror of the possessed. Yet Kolder played upon this older enmity and fear to make their future victims their present allies.

The nature of Kolder. Simon began to concentrate upon that. Their native civilization was a mechanical, science-based one—that fact had been amply proven by what they had found in Gorm. The Estcarpian command had always believed that the Kolder themselves must be few in number, that it was necessary for them to have the possessed captives in order to keep their forces in the field. And now that Gorm was gone and Yle evacuated—

Yle evacuated! Simon's eyes came open, he stared at the ceiling of the cabin. *How* had he known that? Why was he so very sure that the Kolder's only stronghold on the coast was now an empty shell? Yet certain he was.

Were the Kolder now drawing in all their forces to protect their base? Kolder manpower—there had been five left dead in Gorm, the majority in their own apartments—not killed by any sword or dart, but as if they had willed their own dying—or some animating spark, common to all, had failed. But five! Could the death of only five so weaken the Kolder cadre that they would have to pull in all their garrisons?

Hundreds of the possessed had died in Gorm. And then there were their agents in Karsten—Fulk—and the others such as Aldis who were still alive and about their business. Not true Kolder, but natives who had come to serve the enemy—not as mindless possessed, but with wit and awareness. Not one of the Old Race could be so bent to Kolder use; that was why the Old Race must go!

Again Simon wondered at whence that emphatic assertion had come. They had known that the Kolder wanted no Old Race captives for their ranks of possessed. They had suspected that this was the reason, but now it was as clear in his mind as if he had had it from Kolder lips.

Heard it? Did the Kolder have their form of communication such as that he now held with Jaelithe and Loyse? That thought shook him. Quickly Simon sent a warning to she who followed and caught her unease in return.

"We are sure of the course now," she told him. "Break. Do not send again unless there is great need."

"Great need . . ." That echoed in his mind, and then Simon became aware that the vibration which had been so steady in the walls about him was muted, humming down scale as if the speed they had maintained was being cut. Had they reached their port?

Simon sat up on the bunk, faced the door. Would they lock him with the same stiff control which had kept him prisoner before? He had no weapons, though some skill in unarmed combat. But he hardly thought that the Kolder would try a scuffle man to man.

He was right, even as the door to the cabin opened, the freeze was on him. He could move—by another's will —and he did, out into the narrow corridor.

Men there, two of them. But looking into their eyes Simon controlled a shudder only because he could not move save an order. These were possessed, the dead alive of the Kolder labor horde. One was Sulcar by his fair head, his height; the other of the same yellow-brown skinned race as the officer who had brought Simon on board.

They did not touch him, merely waited, their soulless gaze on him. One turned and started along the passage, the other flattened back against the wall to allow Simon by, and then fell in behind him. Thus, between the two, he climbed the ladder, came out on the surface of the submarine.

Above was an arch of rock. The water lapped sullenly against a waiting quay and Simon saw here a likeness to the hidden port beneath Sippar, evidently a familiar pattern for the enemy. Still moved by remote control he walked ashore on the narrow gangway.

There was activity there. Gangs of almost naked possessed shifted boxes, cleared spaces. They worked steadily, as if each man knew just what was to be done, and the quickest way of doing it.

No voices raised, no talk among the work gang. Simon stalked stiffly behind his guide, the Sulcar bringing up the rear, and no one looked at them. The quay was long and two other subs nosed against it. Being unloaded Simon noted. Signs of withdrawal from other posts?

Before them were two exits, a tunnel and a flight of stairs to the left. His guide took that way. Five steps and then a waiting cubby. Once they were inside the door closed and they arose in an elevator such as had been in Sippar.

The ride was not long, the door slid open upon a corridor. Sleek gray walls with a metallic luster to their surfaces, outlines of doors, all closed. They passed six, three to a side, before they came to the end of the hall and a door which was open.

Simon had been in the heart center of Sippar and he half expected to see here again the seated Kolder, the capped master at a cross table, all the controls those men had run to hold their defenses tight.

But this was a much smaller room than that. Light, a harsh burst of it, came from bars set in the ceiling in a complicated geometric pattern Simon had no desire to examine closely. The floor had no discernible carpeting, yet it yielded to cushion their steps. There were three chairs, curved back and seat in one piece. And in the center one a true Kolder.

Simon's guards had not entered with him, but that compulsion which had brought him out of the submarine now marched him forward a step or two to face the Kolder officer. The alien's smock-like over garment was the same gray as the chair in which he sat, as the walls and the flooring. Only his skin, pallid, bleached to a paper white, broke that general monotone of color. Most of his head was covered by a skull cap, and as far as Simon could see, he had no hair.

"You are here at last." The mumble of an alien tongue and yet Simon somehow understood the words. Their meaning surprised him a little, one could almost believe that they were not captor and prisoner but two who had some bargain in prospect and needed only to come to a final agreement. Caution kept Simon silent—the Kolder must reveal his game first.

"Did Thurhu send you?" The Kolder continued to study Simon and now the other thought that there was a spark of doubt in that question. "But you are not an outer one!" The doubt flared into hostility. "Who are you?"

"Simon Tregarth."

The Kolder continued to hold him with a narrowed stare.

"You are not one of these natives." No question but an assured statement.

"I am not."

"Therefore you have come from beyond. But you are *not* an outer one, and certainly not of the true breed. I ask you now—what are you?"

"A man from another world, or perhaps another time," Simon saw no reason not to tell the truth. Perhaps the fact that he was a puzzle for the Kolder was to his advantage.

"What world? What time?" Those shot at him harshly.

Simon could neither shake his head nor shrug. But he put his own ignorance into words.

"My own world and time. Its relation to this one I do not know. There was a way opened and I came through."

"And why did you journey so?"

"To escape enemies." Even as you and yours did, Simon added in his mind.

"There was a war?"

"There had been a war," Simon corrected. "I was a soldier, but in peace I was not necessary. I had private enemies—"

"A soldier," the Kolder officer repeated, still appraising him with that unchanging stare. "And now you fight for these witches?"

"Fighting is my trade. I took service with them, yes."

"Yet these natives are barbarians, and you are a civilized man. Oh, show no surprise at my guess, does not like always recognize like? We, too, are soldiers and our war brought us defeat. Only it has also brought us victory in the end since we are here and we hold that which shall make this world ours! Think you on that, outsider. A whole world to lie thus—" He stretched forth his hand, palm up, and then closed his fingers slowly as if he balled something tangible within his fist. "To serve as you will it! These natives cannot stand against what we have to back us. And—" he paused and then added with slow and telling emphasis, "we can use such a man as you."

"Is that why I am a prisoner here?" Simon countered.

"Yes. But not to remain a prisoner—unless you will it. Simon Tregarth, March Warder of the south. Ah, we know you all—the mighty of Estcarp." His expression did not change, but there was a sneer in his voice.

"Where is your witch wife now, March Warder—back with those other she-devils? It did not take her long to learn that you had nothing she cared to possess, did it? Oh, all that passes in Estcarp, Karsten and Alizon is known to us, to the minutest detail it is known. We can possess you if we wish. But we shall give you a choice, Simon Tregarth. You owe nothing to those she-devils of Estcarp, to the wandering-witted barbarians they control with their magic. Has not that witch of yours proved to you that there can be no loyalty with them? So we say—come with us, work in our grand plan. Then Estcarp will lie open for *your* plucking, *your* terms—or strike any other bargain you wish. Be March Warder again, do as Estcarp wishes, until the word comes to do otherwise."

"And if I do not accept?"

"It would be a pity to waste one of your potential. But he who is not with us is against us, and we can always use a strong back, legs, arms to labor here. You have already tasted what we can do—your muscles do not obey you now, and you cannot take a step unless we will it so. This can be used otherwise. Would you care to breathe only by our favor?"

There was a sudden constriction about Simon's chest. He gasped under that squeezing pressure and panic awoke in him. Less than a second, but the fear did not leave him when he was released. He did not in the least doubt that the Kolder could do as was threatened—keep the air from his lungs, if they chose.

"Why . . . bargain?" he gasped.

"Because the agents we wish cannot be forced. Under such controls you must be constantly checked and watched, you would not so serve our purpose. Accept freely and you will be free—"

"Within your limits," Simon returned.

"Just so. Within our limits, and that will remain so. Do not believe that you can give assent with your lips and keep to your own purpose thereafter. There will be a change in you, but you will retain your mind, your personality, such of your desires and wishes as fit within the framework of our overall plan. You will not be only flesh to carry out orders as those you term possessed and you will not be dead."

"And I must choose now?"

The Kolder did not answer at once. Again his expression was blank, but Simon caught a faint tinge of meaning in his voice—threat, uncertainty, maybe one and the same.

"No—not yet."

He made no signal which Simon could distinguish but the control brought him about, set him walking. No guards this time, but they were not needed. There was no possible way for Simon to break free, and the threat of constriction about his chest was with him still, so that every time he thought of that he had the need to breathe deeply.

Down the corridor, into the elevator again. Up, an open door; the order to move, another hall and another door. Simon went into the room beyond and the control was gone. He turned quickly, but the door was closed and he did not need to try it to know that it would not open.

The harsh, artificial light of the lower room was gone. Two slit windows were open to the day and Simon went to the nearest. He was in a position of some height above a rocky coastline with a sheer descent to water. By side glimpses he got an idea of the building; it must resemble Yle. Not only was the window slit too narrow to climb through, but there was no way down, save that drop straight to the sea-washed rocks.

Simon crossed to the other window. Bare rocks again, not the slightest sign of vegetation—rocks in wind-worn pinnacles, in table mesas, slashed into sharp-walled canyons and drops. It was the most forbidding stretch of natural territory he had ever seen.

Movement. Simon pushed forward as far as he could in the window slit to see what moved in that tormented wilderness of broken rock. A land machine of some sort, not unlike a truck of his own world, though it progressed on caterpillar tracks, which crunched and flattened the surface at a pace, Simon judged, hardly faster than a brisk walk. There were marks on that surface which the machine followed. This was not the first truck which had gone that way, or perhaps not the first trip this one had made in the same direction.

It had a full cargo and clinging to that lashed-on gear, were four men, their ragged scraps of clothing labeling them slave laborers. The machine lurched and jerked so that they held with both hands and feet. That slow crawl inland with a cargo on board. Simon continued to watch until the truck disappeared behind a mesa. It was only then that he turned to examine his new prison.

Monotone color and a bed which was merely a shelf opening from the wall and covered by a puffed, foamy substance. Closed doors of cupboards—a whole row of them. One upon his investigating turned down into a table, another gave him sanitary arrangements as there had been on the submarine. The rest remained tightly closed. It was a room to induce boredom, Simon thought. Perhaps its very monotony was a piece of careful contrivance.

But there was one thing he was sure of: this *was* the Kolder base. And there was a good chance that they might have him under some form of observation. The fact that he had been released from control might even be because they wished to see how he would use his freedom. Could they suspect the tie? Was he bait in a trap to bring in Jaelithe?

What would the Kolder give to have one of the witches in their hands? Simon thought that under the circumstances they would give a great deal. Suppose that everything—*everything*—which had happened to him since the awakening in Tormarsh when he had found Jaelithe again had really been of their engineering! He could not be sure it was not.

Yet the Kolder depended upon their machines. They affected to despise the power. So had they any way of detecting what Simon, Jaelithe and Loyse had woven? To contact Jaelithe now . . . would it be right or wrong? Betrayal or report? He had promised to let her know when he reached the base, give her the news which would eventually summon Estcarp. But how long would it take to bring in that armada? And what could darts and swords or even the power, do against the weapons the Kolder must mount here—things which had not perhaps been in Gorm or Yle? Should he call or stay silent?

More movement. A truck crawling back. Was it the same vehicle he had watched depart? But that hardly would have time to unload and this was empty.

Call—or be silent? Simon could no longer use this useless survey of the land as an excuse for not making up his mind. He went to the bed, lay down upon it. A chance—but everything was a chance now, and if this was not betrayal, then he dared not delay.

14 WITCH WEAPON

JAELITHE HAD journeyed on Sulcarships before, but never into the void of mid-ocean. There was a vast impersonality about the sea which undercut her confidence in herself in a way she had never known before. Only the knowledge that her witchdom had not been swept away was her support. The witches had the reputation of being able to control natural forces. Perhaps on land they could summon up a storm, a mist or weave hallucinations to control the mind. But the sea was a power in itself and the farther the *Wave Cleaver* sailed the less sure Jaelithe was.

Simon's fear that they might have awakened the suspicions of the Kolder, oddly enough, steadied her. Men

—even the Kolder, alien as they were—she could face better than this rolling immensity of wind-driven wave.

"There is no land reckoned hereby on any chart." Captain Stymir had out his rolls of sea maps.

"Have none of your exploring ships ever reached in this direction before?" Jaelithe asked, seeing in his very bewilderment something strange.

Stymir continued to study the top chart, tracing markings with hs finger. Then he called over his shoulder, "Pass the word for Jokul!"

The crewman who came in answer to that hail was a small man, bent by the years, his brown face seamed and salt-dried. He walked with a lurch and go and Jaelithe saw his right leg was stiff and a little shorter than the left.

"Jokul," Stymir flattened the chart with a broad hand, "where are we?"

The smaller man's head came up. He pulled off a knitted cap so that the wind lay over his tight braids of faded hair, his somewhat large nose pointed into that breeze.

"On the lost trace, Cap'n."

Stymir's frown grew the deeper. He studied the filled sails above them as if their billowing had taken on a sinister meaning. Jokul still sniffed that wind, advancing a step or two down the deck. Then he pointed to the sea itself.

"The weed—"

A thread of red-brown on the green, whipped up and down with the rise and fall of the swell, trailed on near to another patch. Jaelithe's gaze, following that, saw that closer to the horizon there was an all red-brown patch. And the change in the captain's expression made her break silence.

"What is it?"

He brought his fist down with a thumping blow. "That must be it!" His frown was gone. "This is why—the weed and the lost trace!" Then he turned to her. "If your course leads there, lady, then—" His hands were up and out in a gesture of bafflement.

"What is it?" she demanded for the second time.

"The weed, it is an ocean thing, living on the surface of the waves in these warmer waters. We have known it long and it is common. One may find bits of it washed ashore after any storm. But there is this about the weed —it has been increasing and now the patches have that on them which kills—"

"Kills how?"

Stymir shook his head. "We do not know, lady. A man touches it and it is as if his hands are burned in a fire. The burns spread upon his skin, his body, and afterwards, he dies. It is some poison in the weed—and wherever it floats we no longer go."

"But if it is in the water and you are on board ship, do you need to fear the touch?" she countered.

"Let a ship touch it and it clings, clings and grows— aboard!" Jokul broke in. "It has not always been so, lady, only for some years now. So the ocean paths it takes we must now avoid."

"Only lately," Jaelithe repeated. "Since the Kolder have grown so bold?"

"Kolder?" Stymir stared at the floating weed in open bewilderment. "Kolder—weed—why?"

"The Kolder ships go under the surface of the sea," Jaelithe pointed out. "How better could they protect their trail than to sow trouble above where any enemy must follow?"

The captain turned to Jokul. "The lost trace—where did it lead?"

"Nowhere that we wished to go," the crewman answered promptly. "A few barren islands which have nothing. Water, food, people, even the sea birds are scarce there."

"Barren islands? Are they not on your chart, Captain?"

He flattened out the top one again. "Not so, my lady. But if this is the lost trace, then it may be that we cannot follow it farther. For the nature of the weed is such that first it appears in such strings as yonder, then in patches, as you see farther beyond. These patches thicken, not only in number but in depth, so that they make small islets borne on the sea, and then larger islets, and at last, if anyone has the folly to push in, they are a solid mass. This, too, was not always so. The weed made islands, aye, but not so solid—nor was it death to hunt there. I have harvested crabs for the eating. But now no man goes near that ocean stain. Does it not seem as blood washing from a gaping wound? The very sign of the death it is!"

"If one cannot penetrate so far how does one know of these isles?"

"At first we did not know the danger. A floating ship with dying men on her deck drifted out of the weed. And of those who chanced upon that vessel and went to their rescue five more died because the weed had fastened to her hull and they had brushed against it. So did we learn, lady. If the Kolders have indeed set this defense about their hold, it is one we cannot face unless we work out some plan against the weed."

The floating weed—Jaelithe had to accept their word upon its danger. The Sulcar kind knew the sea and all its concerns—that was *their* mystery. The weed . . . But she no longer saw that trail like blood on the sea. Her hands went to her head and she swayed at an imperative summons. Simon!

Simon in the Kolder base—that way—beyond the floating death. They must head into—through—that.

"Simon," her reply sought him urgently, "there is danger between us."

"Stay off! Do not risk it."

Curtain between them now. She could not penetrate that despite frantic efforts. Kolder curtain. Did they *know*, or was that only usual precautions? Simon!

Jaelithe felt as if she had screamed that name, it was a

tearing pain in her throat. But when she opened her eyes Stymir showed no alarm.

"What we seek lies beyond there," she said dully, pointing to the horizon where rode the weed. "Perhaps they also know that we come—"

"Captain! The weed!" Not a warning from Jokul, but a cry from the mainmast lookout.

One trail—one patch. No! A dozen trails now, all reaching out deadly tendrils for them. Stymir roared orders to bring the ship about, send it backtracking. Jaelithe sped for the cage on mid-deck.

The great white falcon welcomed her with a scream as she clicked open the latch of the cage. She stiffened her arm to support its weight as it hooked its heavy claws about her flesh and bone, sidled out to freedom. Fastened to one of those strong legs was what she sought, a tiny mechanism in a rod which the bird could carry with ease. Jaelithe drew a deep breath, to steady her nerves and quiet the racing of her heart. This was a delicate business and she dared make no mistakes. Her finger nail found the tiny indentation in the rod, and she pressed that in code pattern. The bird in flight would automatically register, on this triumph of the Falconers' devices, the course and distance. But the tale of the weed was another matter which she must record for the Falconers to decode.

That done she carried the bird to the afterdeck, speaking to it softly meanwhile. Falconers' secrets remained secrets as far as their allies were concerned. How much the bird actually understood Jaelithe could not tell. Whether it was training or bred intelligence which made this falcon superior was a matter for argument. But that it was their only chance to warn the fleet following she knew.

"Fly straight, fly fast, winged one." She drew a finger down the head as those fierce eyes met hers. "This is your time!"

With a scream the falcon tore skyward, circled the ship once, and then shot as a dart back towards the long-vanished land. Jaelithe turned to the sea. The tendrils of weed advanced, a swelling web of them reaching for the ship. Surely, surely their rapid drawing in upon the vessel was not natural. How could floating weed move so swiftly and with a purpose, as she was sure was happening now. Oh, if she only had her jewel! There was more than hallucinations to be controlled through that. At times of great emergency it could pull upon a central store of energy, common to all the witchdom of Estcarp, and so accomplish tangible results.

But she had no jewel, and what she could use was not the power she had known before. Jaelithe watched the fingers of the weed and tried to think. It lay upon the surface—and so far there were no thick islands such as Stymir had feared. Under the water was safe, but the *Wave Cleaver* could not go below as did a Kolder ship.

Water gave the stuff support and life. Her fingers moved in a studied pattern on the rail before her. Jaelithe found herself reciting one of the first and earliest of the spells she had ever learned: one to impress upon a child's mind the base for all "changing."

"Air and earth, water and fire—"

Fire—the eternal opposition to water. Fire could dry water, water could quench fire. Fire—the word lingered with a small beat in her mind. And Jaelithe knew that beat of old, the sign every witch waited for, the signpost of a spell ready to work. Fire! But how could fire be the answer on the ocean—a weapon against drifting weed which was poison to what it touched?

"Captain!" She turned to Stymir. He scowled at her as if she was only a distraction in his battle to save his ship.

"Sea oil—you have sea oil?"

His expression changed to one of a man facing a hysterical woman, but she was already continuing.

"The weed, will it burn?"

"Burn—on the water?" His protest was halted as if a thought struck home. "Sea oil—fire!" He connected those with the rapidity of a man who had improvised before in the face of danger. "No, lady, I do not know whether it will burn—but one can try!" He shouted an order.

"Alavin, Jokul, get up three skins of oil!"

The skins of thick oil, skimmed from the boil off langmar stems, kept for use in storms, were brought to the deck and Stymir himself made the small cuts on their upper surfaces before they were lowered on lines to drag behind the *Wave Cleaver*. The oil began to ooze forth some distance from the ship.

It showed as a distinct stain on the waves, spreading as the leaking bags were rolled and mauled by the force of the waves. When that dark shadow made a goodly streak, one of the marines went aloft. His dart gun had been checked by Stymir and a round dozen in the clip load were the burst-fire type, used to set aflame an enemy's rigging and sails.

They watched the patch eagerly. The strings of weed had reached it, had pushed on so that weed was discolored. There was a burst of eye-searing white fire on one of those soggy tendrils. Soaring flames licked along the oil slick—from more than one place now as the marksman placed his darts.

Smoke rose in a haze and the wind drove to them a stench to set them coughing. Flames roared higher and higher. Stymir laughed.

"More than oil feeds that! The weed burns."

But would more than just the oil-soaked tendrils burn? That was the important question now. Unless those branches of weed ignited and the fire spread to the other patches, they had not gained more than a small measure of time, a very small measure.

If she only had the jewel! Jaelithe tensed, strained against the bond of impotence. Her lips moved, her hands cupped as if she did hold that weapon. She began to sing. No one had ever understood why the gems worked to focus the magic wrought by will and mind. If their secret had once been known to her people, it lay so far back in the dim corridor of their too-long his-

tory as to be buried in the dust of ages. The making of
the jewel itself, the tuning of it to the personality of she
who was to wear it, probably for the rest of her life, that
they could do. And the training of how to use it proper-
ly, that was also a matter of lessoning. But *why* it worked
so and who first discovered this means . . .

The archaic words of her chant meant nothing now
either. Jaelithe only knew that they had to be used to
raise the power within her, make it flood her body, and
then flow outward. And, though she had no jewel, she
was doing now what she would have done had it lain on
her palm, pulsating with her song.

She was no longer aware of the captain, of the crew,
even visual and tactile contact with the ship was gone.
Although no mist born of magical herbs and gums
wreathed her in as it must for the difficult raisings, Jaelithe was as blind as if she was so enfolded. And all the
will which seethed within her body, had been bottled
in her since she laid aside the witch gem, was thrust at
the fire, as if she held a spear within her two hands and
aimed it at the centermost point of the flames.

Those were reaching higher and higher into the sky;
then their red tips bent—not towards the ship, but away
—back at the center mass of the weed on the borders of
which they fed. Away and down. Jaelithe's chant was a
murmur of storm afar. They might have loosed a whole
shipload of oil rather than three skins. Stymir and his
crew stood agape at the holocaust spouting behind them.
A forest in full blaze could hardly have produced more
cloud-reaching tongues of flame.

There was a clap of noise and a second before they
were hardly more than conscious of the first.

Jaelithe stiffened, for a moment her voice wavered.
Kolder—Kolder devices within the weed! She aimed
her will—the fire against Kolder blankness. Were there
underwater ships slinking out to do battle? But the fire
continued to bend to her will.

Those sharp explosions were coming faster. Half the

horizon was aflame and the heat of it struck at the ship, the stench of the burning made a gas to set them choking. Still Jaelithe sang and willed, fought for the death of the weed. And the weed died, shriveled, cooked, became ash awash on the waves. Jaelithe knew a swell of triumph, a wild joy which, in its way, could be as defeating as the fire. She fought against that sense of triumph, beat it down with all her might.

No more red trails across the water, the flames had eaten those into nothingness. Now the fire fed on the larger mass behind them. The *Wave-Cleaver*'s crew watched as the day went and night drew in, but still there was a distant glow along the horizon. And then Jaelithe slumped against the rail, her voice naught but a husky croak. Stymir steadied her while one of the men went running for a cup of ship's wine, thin and sour, but wet to ease somewhat the dried agony of her mouth. She drank and drank again, and then smiled at the captain.

"The fire will eat it to the end, I think," she said in the whisper which was the only voice left her.

"This was great magic, lady." And the respect in his voice was that a Sulcarman kept for some great feat of seamanship or notable stroke in battle.

"How great you do not know, Captain. The oil and the fire darts gave it birth, but the shaping by will set it deep. And—" She raised her empty hands and stared at them now with wonder, "And I had no gem! I had no gem!" She strove to stand away from Stymir and staggered, as weak as one risen from a sick bed of long enduring.

The captain half led, half carried her below, helped her to stretch out on the bunk, where she now lay, trembling with a terrible fatigue. She had felt nothing such as this since her earliest days of training. But before she lapsed into the unconsciousness which lapped about her as the sea lapped the ship, Jaelithe caught at Stymir's hand.

"Do you now sail on?"

He studied her. "This may be only the first of their

defenses and the least. But after what I have seen—aye—
for now we sail on."

"If there is trouble—call—"

Now there was a smile about his lips. "Be very sure of
that, lady. A man does not hesitate to use a good weapon
when it lies to hand. And we still have several skins of
oil below."

He left and she pillowed her head with a sigh of half
content, too tired now to examine this new knowledge,
to taste it, feel it warm about her like a cloak against the
chill of a winter storm. She thought that her tie with
Simon had been her new skill, but it would seem there
was another—and there could be more to discover. Jaelithe stretched her aching body and fell asleep, smiling.

15   MAGIC AND—MAGIC

SIMON STOOD at the seaward window of his prison cell.
Along the horizon now there was no night such as hung
over the rock perch of the Kolder fortress, but a curtain
of living fire reaching from the sea to heaven, as if the
very substance of the ocean unnaturally fed that flame.
Every nerve and muscle in him wanted action. Behind
that wall of fire somewhere—Jaelithe! But there was no
tie between them. He had only her last message, which
was in part a cry for help. This was some Kolder trick.
No wooden-walled Sulcar ship could dare push through
that barrier.

Yet, there was a stir along the cliffs below, a buzz of
activity at the seashore where those who served Kolder
stood to watch the distant flames. And once Simon was

sure that he had seen a true Kolder there, gray smock, capped head, as if what was happening out at sea had so much import that one of the masters must see for himself and not depend upon reports from inferiors.

There had been activity on the land side, too. More of the caterpillar vehicles crawled out into the wilderness of the tortured rock, now with broad beams of light fanning out before them to mark the safest path across the rough terrain. And Simon was sure that he could make out a haze of more light beyond, rising from behind the mesa some miles away.

The Kolder were in haste. But there could be no armada of Estcarp yet at sea. At least no fleet near enough to threaten this keep. And the fire would hold any off a while. So, why all this step-up? No one had approached him since he had been sent here. He could only watch and guess. But only one answer fitted for Simon. The Kolder were under pressure—and time supplied that pressure. Whatever they did which was so important lay in the interior. And that could be their gate! Did they contemplate a return to their own world? No—the Kolder wanted power in this one, and they proposed to gain that by the aid of superior arms, though their numbers must be very few. So, did they wish to recruit from beyond that gate—or bring out new weapons?

But they had been driven out of their own world. Would they dare venture back? More likely they strove to bring out more of their own kind.

He bent his head to rest his forehead against the cool wall and tried again, vainly, to reach Jaelithe. The need for knowing how she fared was as great as his desire for action. But—Kolder blankness there . . .

Loyse! Where in this pile was Loyse? As he had not had any touch with the girl since he had been here he did not know. Now Simon fixed his mind on Loyse, called her.

"Here—"

Very faint, wavering, but still an answer. Simon concentrated until that effort became pain. Their contact had never been clear, it was like trying to clasp in his hands an elusive fog which weaved and ebbed, slipped between his fingers.

"What chances with you?"

". . . room . . . rocks . . ." Contact faded, renewed, faded again.

"Jaelithe?" He asked without much hope.

"She comes!" Much stronger, carrying conviction.

Simon was startled. How did Loyse know that? Tentatively he tried again to reach Jaelithe; the barrier held. But Loyse had seemed so sure.

"How do you know?" He made a sharp demand of that.

"Aldis knows—"

Aldis! What part did the Kolder agent play in this? And how? A trap being set? Simon asked that.

"Yes!" Clear again, and forceful.

"The bait?"

"You, me . . ." Again an ebb and when Simon tried to pursue that farther, no answer at all.

Simon turned away from the window to look about the room. He had investigated its possibilities when he had been sent here. There was no change. But still he must do something—or go mad! Somewhere there had to be a way out of this room, a way to stop the Kolder trap.

The cupboards which had remained obstinately shut to his earlier search— Simon set himself to the task of remembering all he had learned concerning the Kolder headquarters in the heart of Sippar. He had found living quarters there also, hidden out in them after he had escaped the horrors of that laboratory where the possessed were fashioned from living but unconscious men. And there also had been cupboards and drawers which defied his opening.

But there had been one mechanical device within the fortress which the Estcarpian invaders had learned to use, first in awe, and then as matter-of-course: the elevator which ran on the power of thought direction. One designated the floor mentally and arrived there promptly. An engine may have supplied the power, mind supplied the directive. In fact, had not mental control existed throughout Sippar? That Kolder leader with the metal cap wired to the installations, whose death had meant the death of the hold in turn—he had been thinking life into the other world machines. So mind ran the Kolder installations.

And in Estcarp the witches' power was really mental; they could control the forces of nature by thought—without the intermediary of the machines the Kolder depended upon. Which meant that witch power might be the stronger of the two!

Simon's hands balled into fists. He could not face the Kolder with hands, he had no weapons, which left him only his mind. But he had never tried to fight in that fashion. Jaelithe—even the Guardians had conceded —that he had strength in that way which no male of this world had ever displayed. But it was a pallid thing compared to the energy which the witches were able to foster, trim, turn, use— And he had had no training in its use, save that which conditions had forced upon him these past few months.

Simon looked from his useless hands to the cabinets in the wall. He might be battering his mind and will uselessly against an unbreakable barrier, but he had to do *something!*

So—he willed. He willed a door to open. If there was some mechanism within which would answer to thought, then he willed it to yield to him. He visualized a lock such as might exist in his own world, then he went through the steps of unlatching. Perhaps the alien mechanism was so unlike what he thought of that his efforts would have no effect. But Simon fought on, until he swayed dizzily on his feet, stumbled to the bunk and sat there. But never did he take his eyes from that door, from the movements of the lock which must answer his will!

He was trembling with effort when the panel moved and he looked into the interior of the cupboard. For a moment he sat where he was, hardly able to believe in his success. Then he went forward on his knees, ran his hands about the door frame. This was no self-deceiving hallucination—he had done it!

What lay inside could not provide him with either the means of escape or a weapon. A pile of small boxes, which when opened held narrow metal strips coiled into tight rolls, series of indentations along their surfaces making Simon believe them records of sorts. But it was the method of lock he wanted most to see. Lying on his back, putting his head into that cubby, using fingers to help his eyes, Simon gained some idea of the mechanism.

Now Simon sat up to face the second cupboard. No exhausting struggle this time. When the second door opened he looked in at what might be his passport for exploration outside this room. Kolder clothing was stored in transparent bags.

Unfortunately the owner was smaller than Simon. When he pulled on the gray smock he found that it did not reach far past his knees and was bindingly tight about the shoulders. But still it might serve after a fashion. Now—the room door.

If it just worked on the same principle as the cupboards— With the Kolder smock about him Simon turned to face that last barrier. Outside the night was solidly black, but there was a dim glow coming from the walls. Simon thought of the lock . . .

Open! Slide open!

An answering click. The portal had not rolled away as did the cupboards, but it gave when he pushed. With the ill-fitting clothes on him, Simon looked into the corridor. He remembered how in Sippar a voice had come from the air, as if his movements had been monitored. The same could exist here, but he could not know. He walked out into the hall, listening.

Using the elevator which had brought him here he could return to sea level, but that would also take him into the center of activity. What he wanted was to be out of the hold entirely. Loyse. Frowningly Simon considered the problem of Loyse. Aldis and Loyse—the latter to be used as bait for Jaelithe. But where in this pile could he find the girl. He dared not trust mind contact again.

Four more doors along this hallway—it could be that they put their prisoners close together. What had Loyse said? ". . . room . . . rocks." Which might well mean that her windows gave her sight of the rocky interior. His room had been the sea and interior, but the two rooms now to his left would have outlet only for the rocks.

Simon tried the panel of the first door. It moved under his touch for an inch or so and he stepped quickly to the next. They did not give. He drew one finger tip along its resistance and thought. A locked door did not necessarily mean that Loyse was behind it—a big mistake could be made either way.

He concentrated on the lock. It was far easier now that he had the pattern fixed. And his confidence grew. Within the Kolder keep he was no longer a prisoner. With that freeze they could take over his body; could he defeat that now as he could their simpler safeguards? Simon did not know—nor did he long to put that to the test.

The door moved when he tried it the second time. Slowly he pushed it into the wall at his right. Loyse stood with her back to him, her hands on the sill of the window, staring out into the night. And she looked very small and drawn together, as if hunching her thin shoulders and stooping, made her less vulnerable to what she feared.

In Simon's path of vision she was alone, but of that

he could not be sure. Now he attemped another use of his new found strength, willing her to turn and face him. There was a soft cry as she came about, as if she could not stay her movements. Then, sighting him, her hands came up to cover her face and she cowered back, as if she longed to sink into the surface of the wall.

Simon, startled by her reaction, stepped on in and then thought of his smock. She must believe him one of the Kolder.

"Loyse—" He kept that to a whisper, pulling off the tight fitting skull cap of the Kolder disguise.

Simon could see the shudder which shook her, but she dropped her hands, did look at him. Then fear became astonishment. She did not speak, instead she launched herself from the wall, running to him as she might have run for sanctuary. Her fingers gripped the smock where it strained over his chest, her eyes were wide, her lips thinned against her teeth as if to choke back a cry.

"Come!" Simon's arm tightened about her shoulders as he pulled her into the corridor. A moment to close and relock the door, then to choose their way.

But all he knew of the hold were two hallways—this one and that below leading to the room where the Kolder leader had interviewed him. The lower stories of this rat-held warren must be alert and alive with those dispatching supplies and men to the interior. His Kolder disguise would not pass more than the most casual glance. But, those workers on the dockside—the possessed. They had paid no attention to him and his guards when he had landed from the ship, would they be as unnoticing now if he and Loyse ventured among them? And did that port have any outer door?

"Aldis!" Loyse held to his arm, both of her hands braceleting his wrist in a fierce grip.

"What of her?" They were at the elevator, but he could only send it and them into danger.

"She will know that I am gone!"

"How?"

Loyse shook her head. "The Kolder talisman—it is somehow aware of me. That is how she followed the thought path, learned of Jaelithe. She was with me when we made contact. She has a watch on my thoughts!"

After his own experiences Simon dared not scoff at that idea. But he could not summon the elevator without better idea of where to go. There was one place— again a gamble, perhaps the biggest of all. But if Loyse was right and the hunt might be up almost at once, he knew of no better battlefield.

Simon pushed the girl ahead of him. He pictured the corridor which led to the Kolder officer and the door closed behind him. Then he spoke to Loyse.

"Do you feel her? Can you tell when she is in contact and where she is now?"

She shook her head. "No, she is part of their new plan. They want Jaelithe—a witch. And when they found she followed us they were excited. They knew there was a surface ship out there but of that they were not afraid. But something went wrong with their defense and then they made this plan. Aldis was pleased." Loyse was grim. "She said everything was working for them. But why are they so excited—Jaelithe is no longer a witch."

"Not in the manner as before," Simon told her, "but could she have kept contact with us had she no power at all? There is magic and magic, Loyse." But could his magic and Jaelithe's stand against the full force of Kolder?

A faint whisper and the door opened. Here was the corridor he sought. He and Loyse had taken only a few steps along it when that invisible lock caught him. But they continued to march along, helplessly, towards the waiting Kolder.

Helpless? Simon's mind asked. Had he not solved the problem of the doors in the room above he might not have had the temerity to challenge this. He was under a compulsion controlled by the Kolder. But why could he not master that, too? Would he have the time?

The door panel was open. With Loyse, Simon came face to face with those who waited there. Kolders—two of them—one the officer he had fronted earlier. The other wore a metal cap, his eyes were closed, his head tilted back against his chair, his whole attitude one of deep concentration on something afar from his present company. There were two of the possessed bearing guard weapons, and to one side, Aldis, her attention all for the prisoners, an alert excitement in her slightly parted lips, her shining eyes.

The Kolder officer spoke first. "It seems that you are more then we expected, Warder of the Marches, and that you have certain qualities we did not take into consideration. Perhaps it would have been better for you if you had not. But before all else you are going to help us now. For it also seems true that your witch wife has not left you for good after all, but is coming to your side in trouble, as a proper wife should. And Jaelithe of Estcarp is of importance to us—of such importance that we intend nothing shall go amiss in the plans we have for her. So, let us be about the accomplishing of those plans."

Simon's body obeyed that other will. He turned for the door, the two guards again before and behind him. Then came Aldis, the whisper of her robe was unmistakable. The Kolder, too? Only one, he discovered as they reached the elevator. The man in the metal cap remained behind.

Down again. But within the bonds of the control Simon was flexing his new sense of power, beginning to test that compulsion as a man might chip away here and there at some confining shell, seeking the weakest point of its surface. By the time they had reached the water level he was ready for his great effort; however, he reserved that until the proper moment.

The quays were now empty, the undersea vessels there—four of them—inert, nosed against the dock as if they were now useless. And all the laborers were gone. But Simon's party heading on around the water came to a slit in the rock in which steps had been chiseled and they climbed until the air of night and the open shore blew in on them.

Still Simon marched, and then Loyse and Aldis, the Kolder officer to the rear. That fire which had made a scarlet line across the horizon was gone. Though drifts of smoke still arose to cloud the low-hanging stars. The ground here was rough, a scrap of beach walled with many rocks. And this was their final goal. Simon and Loyse faced about. He could not see the guards, but they were there.

"Now—" The Kolder officer ordered Aldis. "Use the girl!"

Simon heard Loyse cry out in pain and terror. He felt the brush of the mental command against his own mind. But at that moment he also struck. Not for his body freedom, not against Aldis or her master here, but at the metal-capped man they had left behind. All the will which had freed Simon from the room locked into a single dart, thrust at the alien. If he had drawn the right conclusions that was the proper focal point.

There was resistance—he had not expected it to be otherwise. But perhaps the very unexpectedness of that assault carried him past barriers too late alerted. Confused thoughts, then rage, finally fear—fear and a quick counter-attack. Only that hampered defense had come too late. Simon hammered home his will. And—his bonds were gone.

But still he stood stiffly, waiting. . . .

16 GATEWAY

IT EDGED IN through the shadows, another shadow close lying on the sea, its prow pointed for the strand just below their stand. Now Simon could hear the faint hiss of water on oar—no sailing vessel, but a ship's boat making a rash touch on enemy territory. He could make out two—three in the boat and he knew that one was Jaelithe.

Beside him Loyse started forward as if to greet the newcomers, her stride stiff, limited. She was under control. And Simon did not need to see what menace hid in the shadows.

"Sul!" He gave voice to the war cry they had heard so many times in battle and threw himself, not at the girl, but at the watching Kolder.

The alien went down with a startled cry as Simon closed. Then the attacker discovered that if the Kolder used machines and possessed, they could also fight hard to save their own skins. This was no easy knockout but a vicious struggle with a fighter who had combat knowledge of his own. The initial surprise of his spring again gave Simon a small advantage which he used to the uttermost.

How it went on the shore he did not know, all his attention on his fight to take the most dangerous opponent out of the melee. At last that body suddenly went limp under him and he waited, his hands still locked about the Kolder's throat, for any quiver of returning energy.

"Simon!"

Through the blood which pounded against his eardrums he heard that. But he did not loosen his hold on the Kolder, only turned his head a fraction to answer.

"Here!"

She came over rocks and sand, only a dark shape to be seen. Behind her moved others. But she would not have come so unless their struggle, too, was done. Now she was beside him, her hand touching his hunched shoulder. There was no need for more between them—not now, Simon thought with a rich exultation rising within him—or ever.

"He is dead," Jaelithe said and Simon accepted her judgment, rising from the huddled body of the Kolder officer. For a moment he caught at her upper arms, drew her to him in what was not quite an embrace, which he needed to assure himself that this was no dream but truth. And he heard her laugh, that small happy sound he had heard before upon occasion.

"I have me a warlock, a mighty warlock lord!" Her voice was a whisper which could not have carried far beyond the two of them.

"And I have me a witch, lady, with more than a little power!" Into that he put all the pride he felt.

"So having paid tribute," now her tone was light amusement for his sharing, "we advance to realities. What do we have here, Simon? The nest of the Kolder in truth?"

"How many are with you?" Simon did not answer her question, but went to the main point.

"No army, March Warder—two Sulcarmen to row me ashore—and these I am pledged to return to their ship."

"Two!" Simon was astonished. "But the ship's crew—"

"No. Upon them we can not depend until the fleet comes. What is to be done here?" She asked that briskly as if indeed she had captained in a troop of his Borderers.

"Very little." His amusement was irony. "Merely a Kolder fortress to face—and their gate—"

"Lady!" A low but imperative call from the shore.

However, before they could answer, light—an eye-dazzling beam of it, striking to the water, lashing a path along the waves from which steam arose.

"Back!" Simon kept his hold on Jaelithe, drawing her with him into rocks which rose more than their height. He pushed her to her knees with an emphatic order, "Stay!" And ran for the beach.

The boat was still drawn up on the shingle, a body lying by it. There were startled cries.

"Get under cover—back here! Loyse—?"

He heard her answer from the left. "Here, Simon—what is that?"

"Some Kolder deviltry—come!"

Somehow he blundered to her, pulled her along, heard a curse in the Sulcar tongue as other figures followed him.

When they reached the rocky space where he had left Jaelithe, Simon found they were a party of six, two Sulcarmen having dragged a silent third form with them. As one they turned to watch the stormy display on the bay. That light, whatever it might be, cut back and forth with the precision of a weapon designed to make sure nothing alive remained afloat on the surface it now lashed. Under its touch the water boiled and frothed into steaming foam.

On the strand was another fire where the skiff had caught and burned as brightly as if it had been soaked in oil. Simon heard Sulcar curses twice as hot from the man crouched on his right.

But Jaelithe was already speaking into his ear, her voice raised above the crackling of the display in the bay.

"They will come, they are coming—"

Simon caught that warning himself, a tingling in his bones. To get away from the bay was necessary. But where to head in this maze of broken rock? The farther from the Kolder keep for now the better. Simon said as much.

"Aye!" That was the Sulcarman beside him. "Which way then, lord?"

Simon stripped off the Kolder smock since he lacked a belt. "Here." He thrust the end of that into the Sulcarman's hold. "Take off your belt, let your mate take the end of that. Through the dark it is best we go linked. What weapons have you?"

"Dart guns, sea swords—we are marines, Lord."

Simon stiffled a sound which dared not be laughter. Side arms—against the Kolder wealth of weapons in their home arsenal! However, night and the rough ground might aid the fugitives.

They moved out, Jaelithe paired with him, Loyse with one of the Sulcar marines, and the silent Aldis with the last. They had tied her hands, but she had not spoken since they had brought her from the shore, only moving at their pushing. Simon argued against the need of taking her with them, fearing betrayal. But Jaelithe had protested, saying she might have some use.

Their pace, of a necessity, could not be fast, but they were well away from the shore and the burning boat by the time they saw lights gather there, scatter out through the rocks marking a search. Simon kept them behind what cover he could and his precautions proved just. For they were in a pocket between two knife-edged, jutting ridges when that searing light burst over their heads.

The fugitives threw themselves face down, the heat of that ray harsh on their backs, although it whipped well above them. Back and forth across the country-side it played, and they cowered in the cut they had so luckily found. Then it flared on. Simon waited. This shift might be a device to entice them into the open. He sat up to watch the sky, studied the path of the ray as reflected there. At last it vanished. Perhaps the Kolder believed them caught and cooked.

There was one direction in which the enemy would not dare to aim that weapon—towards whatever lay behind the mesa to which he had watched those caterpillar trucks crawl. To head for that would give them some insurance against being wiped out. He told them of that.

"This gate—their gate—you think it lies there?" Jaelithe asked.

"Only a guess, but I believe it a good one. They are either reaching through that again, or preparing to. For some reason they must have contact with their home world."

"And that is where we may also find most of their fighters." One of the Sulcarmen observed.

"It is that—or the fortress. And frankly I would rather be in the open than in that Kolder shell again."

The Sulcarman grunted what might be an assent to that. "Open—that is best. Ynglin, this will be a night to notch on the sword hilt before it is done."

"The sword of Sigrod has already been well notched," his fellow replied. "Lord, do we also take this woman with us?"

"Yes!" Jaelithe answered first. "She is needful to us, how I cannot yet see—but yet she will be needful."

Simon was willing to trust to Jaelithe's instinct in this. Aldis had not even gasped when the heat ray skimmed so close to their hiding place. Whether the Kolder agent was in a state of shock, or whether she was familiar with her masters' weapons and merely waited for nemesis to catch up with the fugitives, Simon could not tell. But he felt uneasy over the talisman she carried and what that might do to entangle them again.

"We should take her Kolder symbol—" He spoke that last thought aloud.

But again Jaelithe countered with: "No—in some way that is a key and it may open doors for us. I do not think it will work so, save when Aldis uses it. But no thing of power is to be lightly discarded. And I shall know if she tries to use it, that I shall surely know!" The confidence in her words was complete, though Simon still had shadowy reservations.

Again linked together they began a slow journey, since none of them denied the wisdom of seeking the bottom of each cut or canyon which led in the general direction of the interior. In the dark Simon was the guide, testing and feeling for each step at times. And their progress was painfully slow.

At intervals they rested and all of them nursed bruises, scrapes, a cut or two, from falls and slips among the rocks. The dawn showed them as grimed and dirty scarecrows. But with the early light also came sound . . .

Flattened on a rock slope they could watch, over the spine of a ridge, a crawling vehicle, its arcs of light cutting ahead to dazzle the fugitives' eyes. Simon sighed wth relief. Hs worst fear had been that they were lost in this wilderness of rock. Now he believed they must be close to what they sought.

This crawler was returning to the keep, empty of supplies. Supplies. Simon swallowed. Food, water—both in this barren country would be found only in Kolder hands. Already the need of water pressed him; it probably was as hard for the others. Five of them and a prisoner—and there the might of the Kolder. Perhaps it would have been simpler to invade the keep.

"Simpler—" Jaelithe's answer was almost a part of his own flow of thought. For seconds Simon did not realize that it was not. "Perhaps simpler, but not the right answer."

He glanced at her where she lay, her mail clad shoulder nearly rubbing against his. With her helm on her head and the loose scarf of metal links depending from it wound about chin and throat, half her face was veiled. But her eyes met his squarely.

"Reading of thoughts?" Again she answered an unvoiced question. "Not quite that, I think, rather that a similar path is followed by us both. You are aware, too, that this is necessary for our venture. And the answer is not safety—not for us—but something far different."

"The gate!"

"The gate," she affirmed. "You believe that these Kolder must have something from there to aid in what they would do in our world. That I believe also, therefore they must not succeed."

"Which depends upon the nature of their gate."

The one which had brought Simon into this world had been a very simple affair—a rough stone between pillars of the same crudely hewn substance. A man sat himself there so—hands at his sides fitting into depressions such as also cupped his buttocks. He then waited for dawn and the gate was open. The guardian of that way had told Simon legends in the hours he had passed of a long night waiting for the dawn. The tales told that this was a stone of great story: the Siege Perilous of Arthur's use, an enchanted stone which somehow read a man's soul and then opened to him the world in which he best fitted.

But whatever gate had let the Kolders through to defile this world had not been that kind. And what five of them could do to close it, Simon had not the least idea. Only Jaelithe was also right—this was the thing which must be done.

They skulked along the heights as the light grew stronger, able to follow the marks of the caterpillar trucks below. One of the marines climbed the mesa wall to scout beyond. The others took turns in sleeping in a hidden crevice. Only Aldis sat, staring before her, her hands, though bound at the wrists, resting tight against the Kolder talisman on her breast, as if such touch brought her strength.

She had been a rarely beautiful woman, but now she aged before their eyes, her flesh thinning until the bones were stark in jaw and cheek, her eyes sunken in ridged sockets. Her tangled golden hair was as incongruous as a girl's wig on an old woman. Since they had begun the march her sight had never focused on any of them; she might have been one of the possessed. Yet Simon thought it was not the quenching of life which made her so, but rather a withdrawal to some hiding place deep within her, from which spirit and life would waken when the need came.

And so, for all her present passivity, she was to be watched—if not feared. Loyse was the watcher and Simon thought she took more than a little pleasure in the knowledge that their roles were now reversed, that it was she who controlled, Aldis who obeyed.

Simon lay with his eyes closed, but he could not sleep. The energy he had expended in the Kolder keep and after, instead of tiring him, seemed to set ferment to working. He had the sensation of one faced with a problem, clues close to hand, and the driving need to solve it. More used to weapons he could hold, touch, this new ability to work mentally kept his mind restless, awoke uneasiness in him. He opened his eyes to find Jaelithe watching him across the narrow cleft in which they sheltered. She smiled.

And for the first time he wondered a little at the form of their meeting. That barrier he had thought so thick, growing thicker, had vanished utterly. Had it ever been there at all? Yes—but now it seemed as if it had existed for two other people, not for them.

She did not touch him by hand, or mind, but suddenly there was a flow of warmth and feeling about him, in him, which he had never experienced before, though he thought he had known the ultimate in union. And under that caressing warmth he at last relaxed, the pitch of awareness no less, but not so taut and binding.

Was this what Jaelithe had known as a witch, what she had missed and then thought she had found again? Simon understood perfectly how great that loss must have seemed.

Scrape of boot on rock— Simon was on his feet, looking to the end of the crevice. Sigrod swung down. He pulled off his tight-fitting, crestless helm, wiped his arm across his sweating face. His cheeks were flushed.

"They are there right enough, a whole camp of them— mostly possessed. They have a thing set up." He was frowning a little as if trying to find the words in his seaman's vocabulary to best describe what he had seen. Then he used his fingers to support description. "There are pillars set so . . ." Forefinger pointed vertically. "And a crosspiece—so." A horizontal line. "It is all made of metal, I think—green in color."

Loyse moved. She jerked aside one of those hands Aldis kept folded over her Kolder talisman, displaying a part of the alien symbol. "Like this?"

Sigrod leaned closer, eyeing the talisman carefully.

"Aye, but it is big. Four—five men can march through at once."

"Or one of those crawling vehicles of theirs?" Simon asked.

"Aye, it will take one of those. But that is all there is to it—an archway out in bare country. Everything else well away from it."

"As if it is to be avoided," Jaelithe commented. "Yes, they must be dealing with strange and powerful forces here. Dangerous forces if they strive to open such a passage."

An archway of green metal, alien technology to be unleashed through it. Simon made his decision.

"You," he nodded to the crewmen, "will remain here with the Lady Loyse. If we do not return within a full day strike for the shore. Perhaps there you can find that which will take you to sea and so escape—"

Their protests were ready, he could read them in their eyes, but they did not attempt to deny his authority. Jaelithe smiled again, serenely. Then she stooped and touched Aldis on the shoulder.

Though she did not exert any other direction, the

Kolder agent rose in turn and moved to the end of the crevice, Jaelithe behind her. Simon sketched a half salute, but his words were for Loyse.

"Your part in this is done, Lady. Go with fortune."

She, too, was all protest which she did not utter. Then she nodded.

"To you, also, fortune—"

They did not look back as they began that long tramp, about the base of the mesa so that they might come upon the Kolder camp from the south. The sun was already warm on the twisted rocks about them. It might make this land a furnace before they were out of it. Out of it where? In hiding near the Kolder gate—or—? Somehow Simon was now sure that the gate was not their only goal.

17　BLASTED WORLD

THE SUN was high and, as Simon had foreseen, hot, so that the weight of mail shirt on his shoulders was a burden. He had twisted his Kolder smock about his head turban-wise in place of his missing helm, but the heat beat at his brain as he looked to the Kolder gate. As with the Siege Perilous in Petronius' garden so long ago, he could see nothing beyond it but the same desert of rock. Did this one also need a certain time of day to activate it? He judged that the gate was complete, for no one worked there. Though men lay about the camp site as if struck down in exhaustion.

"Simon!"

Jaelithe and Aldis were in the shadow of a rock pinnacle, sheltered in the only way possible from the glare of this grim waste. The Kolder agent was on her feet, looking not to her companions, but straight out through the shimmering heat waves to the gate. Her hands were again over the Kolder talisman. But her face had come alive. There was an avid eagerness in her expression, as if all she had ever wanted lay just before her for the taking. She began to walk forward at a pace which quickened as she went.

Simon would have intercepted her, but Jaelithe raised a warning hand. Aldis was out in the open now, paying no heed to the heat or the sun, her tattered robe streaming behind her as she began to run.

"Now!" Jaelithe was running in turn and Simon joined her.

They were closer to the gate than those in the camp, and for part of that distance they would be screened from sight as the Kolder party sheltered behind two of the crawler trucks and some of the piled boxes.

It was the gate which was drawing Aldis, and, though she had stumbled and drawn back during their journey about the mesa, she showed no signs of fatigue now. In fact her speed of flight was almost superhuman as she pulled ahead of both her pursuers.

There was a shout from the camp. Simon dared not turn his head for they had come upon a smoothed stretch over which Aldis sped like a winged thing. He doubted if he could match her pace, though Jaelithe was not too far behind her. The gate structure loomed taller in the heat waves.

Jaelithe put on a burst of speed which allowed her to grasp Aldis' torn robe. The fabric ripped the more under her clutch and the other's struggles, but she held fast, although Aldis still pulled her towards the gate. Simon pounded up, his heart beating heavily in his chest, unsteady on his feet from the effort.

Something crackled overhead. Only one of Aldis' wild plunges took them out of the path of that. They were under fire from the camp and in the open they were easy targets. Simon could see only one possible escape. With all his strength he threw himself against both of the women as they struggled, and so rushed the three of them under the crossbar of the gate.

It was plunging from midday into night in a single instant. The sensation of venturing where his kind had no right to go lasted for seconds which were eternity. Then Simon fell into gloom with a lash of rain beating across his body. While overhead crackled such a display of lightning that he was dazzled blind when he raised his head. Jaelithe lay within the circle of his arm and she twisted about, her cheek now close to his.

Water washed about them, dashed into their faces as if they lay in the bed of a swiftly rising stream. Simon gasped and pulled himself up, dragging Jaelithe along. Then she cried out something drowned by the drumming of the storm. By a lightning flash Simon could see that other body, the water striking against it as it lay crosswise, damming the stream. He reached for Aldis. Her eyes were closed, her head rolled limply. Simon thought that he might be carrying a corpse, but he brought her up from the bed of the rapidly filling stream.

They were in a valley between high walls and the water was pouring down very fast. Objects bobbed on its surface, arguing of a flash flood. Simon struggled to the wall and eyed it for possible footholds. They were there but to make that ascent with Aldis was a task which exhausted them both. So that once at the top of the rise he lay again with Jaelithe, his back to the rain, his head pillowed on his arm as he breathed in great sobs.

Neither of the women stirred as at last he levered himself up to gaze about. The sky was dark and the rain continued to pour. Not too far away loomed a bulk promising shelter. Simon shook Jaelithe gently until she blinked up at him.

"Come!" Perhaps she did not hear that word in the fury of the storm but she wavered to her hands and knees and then to her feet with his support. He got her under cover and went back for Aldis.

It was only when he returned that Simon was aware of the nature of their quarters. This was no rock nor crevice cave such as they had used for refuge in the Kolder territory, but a building. Lightning flashes revealed only fragmentary glimpses of the remains. Remains because in the far end of the room in which they stood the roof was partly ripped away, the wall had a great gash down it.

That the break was old was apparent by the straggling bunches of grass which had rooted here and there on the broken flooring. And, in spite of the freshness of the rain-filled wind, there was a musty smell to the whole place.

Simon moved cautiously down the length of the room to that break. There was debris on the floor, twice he nearly lost his footing in a stumble. He trod upon something which crackled and broke under his weight, and caught a glint of lightning flash. With his hands he felt about. Fabric—something rotten which went to slimy shreds, making him wipe his hands on a bunch of grass. Then metal—a rod. Simon picked that up and came back to the doorway where the gloom of the storm seemed lessening, or maybe his sun-dazzled eyes were now adapting to it.

What he held could only be a weapon, he decided. And it bore some resemblances to the rifle of his own world. There was a stock and a barrel. But the metal was lighter in weight than that of any firearm he had known.

Jaelithe had her hand on Aldis' forehead.

"Is she dead?" Simon asked.

"No, she must have hit her head when she fell. This

is the world from which the Kolders came?" There was no fear in her voice, merely interest.

"It would seem so." One thing he was certain of: they must not get too far from this spot, from where they had come through the gate. To lose their way meant perhaps no return.

"I wonder if there is any sign of the gate on this side." As usual now Jaelithe's thoughts had followed his. "They must have some guide if they come through and wish to return again."

The wild storm was dying. The night-darkness which had enveloped them when they had come through the gate was now modified with a gray approaching dawn light. Simon surveyed the terrain with the intentness of a scout. This was not desert such as lay on the other side of the gate. There were evidences of one time occupation of the country all about him, as if this had once been thickly settled land. What he had first believed rocky hills on the other side of the cut, turned out to be the shells and ruins of buildings.

There was a familiarity about all this. He had seen such before when armies had fought their ways across France and Germany years ago. War-torn—or at least visited by some great disaster. And sometime in the past, for vegetation grew among the ruins, rank and high, as if the very destruction of those buildings had provided fertilizer for the plants and shrubs.

No sun showing yet, but the light was that of full day. By that he could see the scars cutting deep into the ruins, where the very ground seemed frozen in a curdled slag, and the nightmare of his own world hovered. Atomic war? Radioactive land? Yet on a closer inspection Simon did not believe so. An atomic bomb would not have left buildings still erect on the edges of those congealed puddles, taken half a structure and spared the balance to stand as a ragged monument. Some other weapon—

"Simon!"

He did not need Jaelithe's alerting whisper for he had

seen that movement behind a ruined wall. Something alive, large enough to be formidable, perhaps on the stalk, was moving in the general direction of the hideout. Jaelithe's hand went to her belt where sword and knife still hung. Simon looked for the weapon he had found on the floor.

Its similarity to a rifle, in spite of its light weight, made him consider it seriously. But the narrow opening in the barrel puzzled him—too small to emit even the needle darts of the Estcarpian sidearms. What *had* been the purpose of that slender tube? Simon held it in firing position. There was no trigger, merely a flat button. And, without believing there would be any result, Simon pressed that.

The bush on which he had sighted the alien weapon shivered, rain water shaking from the leaves. The whole plant quivered and it continued to quiver while Simon watched, hardly believing what he saw. Now the limbs bent earthward, the growth was withering, the leaves shriveling up, the stems twisting visibly. He heard a gasp from Jaelithe as the mass was at last still, a seared and wrinkled lump on the ground. There had been no sound, no visible ray—nothing, save that result of his firing the alien gun.

"Simon! Something coming—" Jaelithe looked beyond the withered bush.

He could see nothing; but feeling—that was different. The sense of danger grew acute. Her hand touched the arm which still supported the weapon.

"Be ready." On the words came another sound from her throat, low—no words—just a murmur.

Cover—three good patches of cover out there. Whatever lurked could hide in all or any. Jaelithe's purring call was louder. He had once seen her spill a Kolder ambush out of hiding; was she trying the same tactics now?

The alert in him was reaching a climax. Then—

From all three covers they came, running silently. One from behind a wall, another from a thick brush, the last from behind a half-fallen building. They were men —or, Simon corrected that as they came into plain sight —they had the general appearance of men. Rags of clothing still covered parts of their bodies, but that only added to the horror, rather than made them more human. For those bodies were thin, arms and legs showing as bone covered with skin, no flesh or muscle underneath. The heads they held high on stick necks were skulls. It was as if the ruins had given up the long dead to stalk the living.

Simon swung up the alien rifle, swept it across that trio. For some heart-choking seconds he thought that the first firing had exhausted whatever strange ammunition that weapon held. Then they halted their silent rush, stumbling only a step or two farther. Their bodies jerked as the bush had quivered.

They were no longer silent, instead there came a thin, high, squealing unlike any human speech, as they jerked and danced, until they toppled to lie still. Simon fought down the nausea which was a bitter taste in his mouth. He heard Jaelithe cry out, and he put his arm about her, drawing her close so they clung together.

"So—"

Both of them were startled by the voice from behind. Aldis, on her feet, one hand steadying her against the cracked wall, came to the door of the building. The smile on her face, as she looked out at the row of doubly dead added to Simon's sickness. It accepted that scene and was pleased by it.

"They still live then—the last garrison?" She paid no attention to either Jaelithe or Simon; they might not have existed. "Well, their vigil is about to end."

Jaelithe moved out of Simon's hold. "Who were these?" She asked in a voice which demanded an answer.

Aldis did not turn her head. Still smiling, she continued to study the dead.

"The garrison—those left to hold the last barrier. Of course, they did not know that that was their only duty—

just to hold while the Command reached safety. They believed, poor fools, that it was only a withdrawal to re-form, that help would reach them. But the Command had other problems." She laughed. "However, this is a surprise for the Masters, for it seems they have held longer than was expected."

How could she know all this? Aldis was not Kolder born. In fact, as far as any knew, there were no women at all among the Kolder. But somehow Simon did not doubt that it had happened just as she said. Jaelithe made a small gesture with her hand as a scout might wave caution.

"There are more—"

Again he did not need her warning. The sense of danger had not greatly lessened. But he could sight no movement about the stretch of open ground before them. And this time Jaelithe did not strive to bring them out. Instead, she turned to gaze at the cut from which they had climbed.

"They gather—but not against us—"

There was a sound from Aldis—not a laugh, but a titter which scaled past the bounds of sanity.

"Oh, they wait," she agreed. "They have waited, a long time they have waited. And now come those who would hunt for us—only there will be a second hunt." Again that titter which was worse than any cry of pain or terror.

But what she said was not insane; it made sense. The Kolder could be coming through the gate to hunt for the three of them. And these—these things—which lingered here were gathering to meet them. Did the Kolder know what they faced?

Simon gave a hasty glance along the edge of the drop. To go out might make them the quarry for those who were moving in, but only so could they see the gate in action. And the nagging fear which had ridden him since they had crashed through had been that return might be denied.

There was a solid-looking base out there, perhaps it

had once supported a superstructure of which only a single rod pointing skyward remained. With their backs to that base they would have a vantage point from which to watch the gate. Cradling the rifle in his arm, Simon caught at Aldis and pulled her along, Jaelithe following fleetly.

What Simon had believed during the storm to be a stream bed now showed as the remnants of a paved road, half covered by falls of debris from the heights. A stream still ran down its middle. A little to the right of their present stand, but down on the level of the road, the wall of the cut, on either side, had blocks of green metal set as pillars.

"The gate," Simon said.

"And its defenders," Jaelithe added in a half whisper.

Those were to be seen now, moving along the cut. For all their unearthly, unhuman aspect, they were setting up an ambush with the cunning of intelligence, or what had been born from intelligence which had once existed. Here and there Simon marked such weapons as the one he held in his own hands.

"They are coming through!"

There was no change in the metal pillars, no sign that the gate was in use, until those men suddenly appeared as if from the air itself. Possessed fighting men, yet they showed caution as they fanned out, moved up the break. There was no hint from those in hiding. And the controlled warriors of the Kolder advanced without facing attack. A full company of them came through, were well along the cut from which every sign of those in ambush had vanished. Now the nose of one of the crawlers appeared, followed by the rest of its ponderously moving bulk. One of the possessed at the controls, but beside him a Kolder agent.

Around, from below, from across the cut, Simon sensed that upsurge—an emotion in the air, dark and heavy.

"They hate—" Jaelithe whispered. "How they hate!"

"They hate," Aldis mimicked her tone. "But still they

wait. They have learned to wait, for that is what they have lived to do."

A second truck crawled out of nothingness. Now the invaders' foot force was well down the old road. This second vehicle had a larger cabin on its body, the top of which was a transparent dome. And in that sat true Kolder, two of them—one wearing a metal cap.

The smoldering cloud of emotion was so strong now Simon expected it to rise as a visible fog. But still those in ambush made no move. A smaller party of possessed, marched stolidly along—labor ready for the need.

Then—nothing more.

"Now!"

Sound, lower than thunder but with a bestial hate which made it one with elements, which owed nothing to intelligence or human understanding. The fury which had been building boiled into action as the possessed shivered, jerked, fell.

There was not enough room in the cut for the trucks to turn. But the one bearing the Kolder officers reversed, crawled backward, so that the possessed who followed it were crushed and broken beneath its treads. Then the driver jerked and quivered in turn. He fell out of sight in the cabin, yet still the truck retreated, or strove to withdraw, though its backward run was now far more unsteady. At last it crashed into one of the piles of debris and slowly tilted, as the treads clawed vainly to keep it upright.

The Kolder wearing the cap had not moved, even his eyes remained closed. Perhaps it was his will which had kept the truck going, even protected him and his fellows now as neither seemed affected by the attack which withered and slew those about them.

His companion turned his head from side to side, studying the route. But no expression Simon could read crossed his white face.

"They have what they want now," Aldis again with that

tittering laugh. "They have caught a master to give them a key to the gate."

They had come out of hiding, those skeletons—the bait of the Kolders drawing them free of caution. Many of them were bare-handed as they swarmed about the truck, strove to climb to the bubble-topped cabin.

Mewling cries—half that company fell back, their bodies blackened, their limbs moving spasmodically. But still more gathered, not quite as unwary now. Until several came together, bearing with them a loop of metallic chain. Three flings before it fell into position about the bubble. Then fire ran around it in a spitting line. When that was pulled away and they climbed again, there was no trouble. The bubble shattered and they were at their prey.

Jaelithe covered her eyes. She had seen the sacking of cities and the things done in Karsten when the Old Race had been horned into outlawry. But this was something she could not watch.

"Only one—" Aldis babbled, "he must be saved for the key—they must have their key!"

The metal-capped Kolder hung limply in his captors' clutches, his eyes still closed. The skeletons were gathering along the cut, to form up as a grotesque demon army behind that captive and those who held him. There were the alien rifles among them, but others had armed themselves with the weapons of the possessed. And their hate was still high and hot. Then, holding the Kolder to the fore, they marched, as if a forgotten training was revived in their union of purpose—for the gate.

Simon moved as the first of them stepped between the pillars and vanished. The Kolder—now these—what evil would be loosed in the world he had come to consider his own?

"Yes, oh, yes!" Jaelithe cried. "A wind, then a whirlwind—and we must face the storm!"

18 KOLDER BESIEGED

ONLY THE DEAD lay in the cut, that sense of alien presence had accompanied that sinister army through the gate. How many had been in that force? Fifty. A hundred? Simon had not counted them, but he believed not over a hundred. And what could so few do against the entrenched might beyond? This was not to be a matter of laying an ambush.

But the Kolder should be too occupied now to remember the fugitives, and this was the time to return with the force before them.

"We go back—"

Aldis gave one of those eerie, tittering laughs. She had crept away from them, was moving along the edge of the ravine, looking at them over her shoulder, a sly grin on her lips. Almost she was coming to resemble the skeletal inhabitants of this land. The last vestiges of beauty had been bleached from her.

"How will you go?" she called. "Door without key, door you cannot batter down. How do you go, mighty warrior and lady witch?"

She was running in a zigzag, fleetly, back into the waste.

"After her!" Jaelithe scrambled by him. "Do you not see? That talisman—it is the key—for her—for us!"

If she were right— Simon followed. Light as it was to carry, the alien rifle was an awkward burden as they smashed through brush. But he clung to it. In spite of the veil of vegetation growing over the debris of the buildings, the ruins were impressive. This had been, if not a city, a fort or settlement of some size. And the number of hiding places among the broken walls were beyond counting. As he and Jaelithe burst into an open space, Simon stopped her with an outthrust arm.

"Where?" He made the one word into a demand and saw her gaze about with dawning comprehension. "She might be within arm's distance or well away, but where?" He hammered home the hopelessness of their unthinking pursuit. This warren of ruins was made for endless hide and seek.

Jaelithe raised her hands and cupped them over her eyes, standing very still while her breathing quieted. Simon did not quite know what she would do, but in confidence he waited. She pivoted, part way around, and then dropped her hands to point.

"Thus!"

"How do—?"

"How do I know? By what is not there—Kolder barrier—and she wears the Kolder talisman."

A thin clue—there could be other Kolder traces in this land. But it was the only one they had. Simon nodded and accepted her guidance. It was a crooked path Jaelithe set them, and it bored on into the mass of ruins away from the cleft. Simon marked a back trail as they went, blazing growths, or scratching stones. But the time this chase was taking he regretted.

They came out on a large paved space, ringed by buildings in a better state of repair than those nearer the cut. There was a different look to these structures—not quite the sealed appearance of the Kolder holds, yet with some of their stark rigidity of design. Grace and beauty in the sense his world knew them, Jaelithe's people held, were totally foreign to the minds which had conceived and built these. And any one of them might provide Aldis with numerous hiding places.

"Where?" Simon asked.

Jaelithe put her hand on the top of a low wall which ran about that open space. Her breath came fast and the dark finger marks of fatigue under her eyes were plain.

172

They had drunk their fill of rain water in the storm, but there had been no food for a long time. Simon doubted if they could hold this pace much longer. And now Jaelithe shook her head slowly.

"I do . . . not . . . know. It has gone from me—" Her hurried breaths were close to sobs. Simon caught her, drew her against him, and she came willingly as if very grateful for his strength, his touch which held comfort.

"Listen," he spoke softly, "do you think you could sing her out, as you did in those in ambush?"

"We must. We must!" Her voice was a husky whisper with an element of hysteria in it.

"And we can! Remember once—back in Kars when there was need of shape-changing and you said that you would call upon me for that which you needed to make the ceremony a swift one? Now it will be the same: call upon me for what you need."

She turned in his arms, though she did not step away from him, only faced outward. And her fingers grasped his in a grip which tightened with her need for the effort. Once more she began to sing that song of invocation which started as a hum and rose higher. And Simon felt, as he had on that day in Kars, that flowing from him, down his arms, through his hands, into her, draining him so he used iron will to stand unmoving.

All this world became one with that sing-song, so that he did not see the drab stones about him, nor the patches of encroaching vegetation—only a kind of silvery sheen which was within him and without him at once and the same time. But there was no time either; only this—this —this—

Then that chant which beat in his veins died, and he saw again this deserted city. There was movement, something in the shadows. Coming into the open, crawling . . . Aldis crawling. She did not try to get to her feet, instead she collapsed and lay still. Jaelithe released her hold on Simon.

"She is dead—"

Simon hurried to turn over the limp body. Blood, his hands were wet with it, yet there was more flowing, so much more. Her wan face was untouched but below, the wound flowed blood.

And torn flesh was one with torn robe where she had worn the Kolder talisman. Jaelithe cried out. But Simon caught at one of the bruised hands which was a fist tightened in death to still protect. He worked the rigid fingers until he released what they had gripped to the end of reason and life. Whatever had striven to tear from Aldis the Kolder device had not succeeded in winning its desire. She had lost her life in that battle, but not what she had fought to retain. He held the talisman.

"Come." Simon stood up, his eyes searching the windows, the doors, for any sign of the one or ones Aldis had met here.

Jaelithe stooped and pulled a fold of the torn robe across the body, veiling the ravaged face and the wound on the breast. Then she made a sign in the air above its quietness.

They worked their way back to the cut at the best pace they could muster. Simon watched the back trail, unable to believe that they would not be stalked by whatever had killed Aldis. Had the possession of the Kolder talisman brought on that assault? He believed that it had, and that it might draw the same fate after them.

The possessed dead lay in the broken road. There was no sign that anyone had passed this way since they had left hours earlier. Only the shadows were longer, the signs of approaching night clear.

They climbed down into the cut and stood on the cracked surface of the road where the wrecked crawler slewed to close it off. There were the pillars marking the gate, the dusk making the green somber streaks. Simon raised his hand, the palm cupping the Kolder talisman, and Jaelithe set her hands on his shoulders, keeping such contact with them as they approached the gate.

Would the talisman take them past? They had been three together when they had made the other crossing. And the skeleton army had needed the Kolder to see them through. Simon walked on.

He did not know what to expect, but he was not surprised when the object in his hand grew cold and colder —this was akin to the Kolder barrier against mind reaching. But Aldis had not been Kolder by blood and it worked for her.

Another step and they were both between those wall strips. Once more the shaking, wrenching sense of being whirled into a nothingness which was highly inimical to their kind—then through it. Simon staggered forward. He was on his hands and knees on rock still warm from the sun of a baking day, Jaelithe beside him.

Sunset was not complete enough to hide what lay before them. There had been a battle here. And it had not all been the way of the other world force as it had on the other side of the gate. The rock was not only heated by sun, great ribbons of black scorch lay back and forth across the whole plain of the gate and there were things lying there . . .

Simon wavered to his feet, stooped to bring Jaelithe up in turn. Nothing before them moved, this had been left to the dead. What he was going to do now might be the wrong thing, but it was the only blow he could see to strike for the freedom of this world against the Kolder and what the Kolder had drawn upon this world.

He raised the alien rifle and fired whatever energy it controlled at the base of the nearer of the gate columns. For a moment in the half light he thought that either the charge was exhausted or that it had no effect upon the structure. Then came a shimmering, licking up from his point of target, running along all that side, coming to the bar at the top, across it, down the opposite pillar. Shimmering became sparkling motes drifting apart.

Simon cried out and dropped the weapon. His hand
—his hand!

The Kolder talisman which had still been in his grasp
when he fired that shot or ray fell from him, leaving his
flesh blackened and burning! It rolled out midpoint between the gate posts shimmering into nothing—to ex-
plode in a flash of green fire. But the gate was also gone
and they looked upon barren space.

Together they staggered on to where the Kolder camp
had been, where there was still a huddle of machines and
about them things neither wished to see clearer; they
were thankful the light was half cut away by the shadow
of the mesa. Simon lurched to the ground by one of the
crawlers, his hand pressed against him, much as Aldis had
always pressed the talisman to her. He was only aware of
the pain, pain mixed with a rising weakness so that he
could not think clearly, pain beyond enduring save for
the space of a breath, and another, and another—

Then the pain was not so great, or else he had become
accustomed to it, as a man might come accustomed to any
torment which lasted. He tasted water and after that a
solid substance was put between his lips and a voice
urged him to eat. How long had he been apart in that
place of pure pain? Simon did not know. But now his
head cleared and he knew that it was dark and nearly as
cold as the day had been hot, that his head rested on
Jaelithe's knee, and that she was striving to wake him,
her voice first only a low murmur and then her words
making sense.

". . . coming. We cannot stay here—"

It was so good just to lie so, the fiery torment in his
hand reduced to a dull pain. Simon strove to move his
fingers and found there was a bandage about them.
Luckily, he thought dreamily, it was his left hand.

"Please, Simon!" More than a plea—a half command.
Jaelithe's hands on his cheeks, gently moving his head
back and forth. Then her arm slipped under his neck,
striving to raise him. Simon protested.

"We must go!" She leaned closer over him. "Please, Simon—there is someone coming!"

Memory flooded back, he sat up. The pool of shadow which had been there when he collapsed was now inky, all light cut off by the bulk of the mesa. He did not question her warning as he pulled himself to his feet, leaning on the crawler's track. For a moment he nursed a dim hope of using the machine, then he knew that he would not understand its controls. Once erect Simon found himself steadier than he had first thought. He moved out with Jaelithe, stumbling over the ruts left by the crawlers.

"Who comes? Kolder?"

"I think not—"

"Those others?"

"Perhaps. Do you not feel it too?"

But if there was anything to be sensed in the night it remained a secret to Simon and he said so. For the first time in many hours he remembered those they had left when they began this last weird adventure. "Loyse—the Sulcarmen?"

"I have striven to reach them. But there are new forces loosed here, Simon, things strange to me. I cannot pierce a barrier, then—suddenly it is gone! Only to rise immediately in another place. It is my thought that Kolder fights for its life, that those who share that blood are using all weapons to their hands—some material, some outside our reckoning. That which came out of the wilderness beyond the gate is still alive to hate, to hunt. And if we do not wish to be caught up in this struggle we must keep aloof. For Kolder fights that which is also Kolder, or what gave birth to Kolder, and this is no war such as our world has seen before."

As he moved on, Simon's strength continued to return. Jaelithe had plundered the camp for rations; she told him of that quietly and he felt her horror of what she had seen on that quest. So again he drew her to him, and they went on with his arm about her shoulders, his bandaged hand resting on her lightly, momentarily content that they could go thus, divided in neither mind nor body.

They were rounding the bulk of the mesa to reach the place where they had left Loyse and the Sulcarmen when a stone, rattling down the side of that table land, made Simon sweep Jaelithe behind him. He had dropped the alien rifle by the gate, but he still had the knife Jaelithe had given him. And now as he listened, that was ready in his good hand.

"Sul—" Not a battle cry but a whisper in the dark.

"Sul!" Simon replied.

More stones fell and then a figure swung down with the agility of a man used to making his way about ship's rigging.

"Sigrod," he identified himself. "We saw you come out of nowhere back there, Lord. But there have been demons in these hills and they destroy aught that moves, so we dared not join you. Ynglin has the Lady Loyse in good hiding and I have come to guide you."

"What has happened?"

Sigrod laughed. "What has not, Lord! These Kolder pushed through that gate and were gone as if they had used a spell for becoming nothing before a man's eyes! Then—why, it was like all Demon Night opening. Out came those others, marching as an army of dead risen out of their graves to bring swords for a cause as dead as they! They came down upon the Kolder camp and —this is the truth I speak, I swear by the Waves of Asper that it be so!—they looked at a man and he shriveled up and died, as if a frost storm or a fire had shot upon him. Witchcraft, Lady, but such as I have never seen in Estcarp.

"They overran the camp as if those within it had not the power to raise hand to sword or shoot a single dart. Then there came the same lightning as strove to seek us out when we left the shore, and that smote and smote again, catching many of the demons and rendering them once more of the earth. But others went on, taking with them a Kolder, and they were traveling toward the sea. Since then there have been strange things in that direction. Only from this height have I seen something to sea. Lady, your sending has been obeyed—for there are sails showing!"

Simon functioned again as a field officer. "And if the fleet runs into that fire—" He put his worry into words. A warning—but how could they deliver that? Would the Kolder, if they were beleaguered in their own hold, weaken their defense to use the lashing fire at a new, sea-borne enemy in a three-cornered fight? And what of the skeletons? Would it make any difference to them whether they hunted Kolder or stood up to a new foe? He must know more of what was going on.

They held council after they joined Ynglin and Loyse in a rock-walled cave.

"There is a way to gain the coast without too much effort," Ynglin reported, "and I, for one, feel the safer with water nearby. This country is too well made for the hunting games which favor the pursuer as well as the pursued. There have been no more fire lashings for some time now. Also we have seen only a few of these wandering bags of bones slinking about. They prowl as if they would sniff up some trail; they do not show the fear of broken men who run from a strong enemy."

"Maybe they have the Kolder besieged in the keep," Simon speculated. "If so—to go seaward might take us into them." He tried to think. The fleet out there—no one ever claimed that Sulcarmen were stupid. They would not run recklessly headlong into a Kolder den, knowing only too well the nature of the enemy and the traps which might lie before them. But this was a good chance, which, if handled right, might stamp out evil once and for all.

He did not believe they could erect another gate in a hurry, not while harassed by these creatures from their own past. Therefore, that retreat was closed to them. A siege. But guesses were not enough; he had to know more and that meant seeing the site of the present activity—the coast and the Kolder keep.

"A scout," he began, when Jaelithe spoke.

"We must go together, all of us. Also, the sea is our answer."

Was that her thought—or his? The sea could be their answer, giving them a chance not only to communicate with the fleet but to scout the Kolder. Simon agreed.

They set out along the way the Sulcarmen had marked during that time when with Loyse they had remained in hiding. It was rough going and in the dusk perhaps doubly dangerous. But night had not yet deepened into full dark and they made the best time they could. The Sulcarmen had raided the Kolder camp before Simon and Jaelithe had returned and the supplies from there, meager as they were, gave them renewed vigor and energy.

Simon took advantage of several rest halts to climb above and try to sight the fleet. At his second failure he commented on that and Sigrod chuckled.

"Aye, they are doubtless coasting. That is a raiding trick which always serves us well. They have split the fleet in twain, each half turning stern to the other. There will be one scouting north and the other south to find a landing."

Simon brightened. He knew next to nothing of naval tactics, and his acquaintance with Sulcar fighting methods had been limited to their service ashore. But this information was helpful. If even one of those divisions now sailing north and south could be contacted . . . He began to question the two marines. They might not be able to reach those now heading north, but the southern half of the fleet was headed in their own direction, and there was an excellent possibility it could be signaled from shore. Ynglin volunteered to try.

Then Simon went on—with the keep as his goal.

19   DRINK SWORD—UP SHIELD

"To SHAKE them out of that, Lord, you will need more than a fleet. Such walls cannot be wished away." Sigrod lay belly down on the rock peak beside Simon regarding the sealed enigma of the Kolder hold.

There was movement below. Apparently those who had come through the gate were gathered before those unscalable, unbreachable walls, willing to wait. Though in a matter of siege Simon thought the Kolder had all the advantage. The force without had no supplies and this was a totally barren land. Perhaps they believed that they would still withdraw through the gate. How long before they discovered that no longer existed?

Wish away walls—that comment remained in Simon's mind. All in all, since he had been here he had seen only four of the true Kolder—the two in the hold and the two who had manned the crawler into ambush. And two of those were dead. Of the others he believed that the one in the cap with whom he had dueled long range from the shore might serve the purpose he was beginning to formulate. *If* that one still lived. But could he be reached and how effective would such a try be? Simon signaled a return to where they had left Loyse and Jaelithe.

They listened to him as he not really outlined any concrete plan, but thought aloud.

"These capped ones—they control the rest?" asked Sigrod.

"At least they give orders and control much of the

installation, of that I *am* sure. The aliens brought one with them; they used him to get through the gate."

"But he did not take them into the keep," Jaelithe pointed out, "or they would not be down there now with the walls held against them."

"He might have been killed in the assault on the camp," Loyse suggested.

"And this other one, whom you fought," Jaelithe continued, "you believe that you can reach him by the power, compel him to do your will?"

"*We* might," Simon corrected.

"So open the doors for those demons?" Sigrod nodded. "But let those get within and the nut is still shelled for our cracking. They were Kolder, too, is that not so, Lord? Then what if we have only exchanged one set of Kolder for another?"

"Yes," Simon admitted the justice of that. "Therefore we hope that Ynglin will be able to bring us reinforcements and we wait."

Much of this warfare with the Kolder was based on waiting, Simon decided. And waiting was the most tiring of all a fighting man's duties—war was full of "hurry up and wait." He rolled over on his back and lay looking up into what was now the thick dark of a cloudy night sky.

"I will take the first watch, Lord." Sigrod started up slope again. Simon grunted assent, still considering the problem ahead, chafing because—as so much else since he had ridden out of the South Keep weeks ago—this must depend on chance. Could one will good fortune or ill? His thoughts slid in another direction. Were the old witchcraft tales of his own world true so one could aim ill luck to strike an enemy as he might fire a dart?

A hand on his forehead, stroking back the sweat-dampened locks of hair which clung damply to his skin.

"Simon." She could always make of his name a singing,

an intimate reaching of one to the other. "Simon—" No more than that, just his name.

He reached up and caught that brushing hand with his unbandaged fingers, brought it down against his cheek and then to his dry lips. There was no need for any more words between them. Theirs had always been an inarticulate love, but perhaps, Simon believed, the deeper for its very wordlessness. And now the last vestige of that barrier between them had vanished. He knew that she had those depths and silences to which she must withdraw upon occasion, that he meant none the less to her because of those withdrawals. They were a part of her and so to be accepted. No one could ever occupy all of another's thoughts and emotions. There were parts of him which would be closed to her also. But to take without question what she did have to give, and offer in return, freely and without jealousy, all he had—that was what their union meant.

"Rest." Her hand went back from his lips to his head, soothingly. Simon knew that she had matched him thought for thought in wordless communication. His eyes closed and he surrendered to sleep.

There was the Kolder keep, sealed as Yle had been sealed, and from this height they could also see the forces from the gate drawn up about it. Nothing had changed during the night.

"They have not used the fire whip again," Sigrod observed.

"Might not dare to so close to their own walls," Simon returned.

"Or else it is exhausted."

"That we cannot count upon."

"They lost a lot of the possessed back there. Too many perhaps to try a sally. How long do you think they will keep sitting here like this?"

Simon shrugged. Could you judge the Kolder by any standard he knew? They might well be able to go without food and water, to squat stubbornly at the enemy gates for days, weeks—

"Simon?"

Jaelithe's face was turned up to his as he looked back and down. Her eyes were alight and there was an eagerness in her expression.

"A sending, Simon! Our people come!"

He glanced at the sea but the bay was free of ships; there were no sails on the horizon. Then he slid down into the hollow behind the scout point. Jaelithe was facing south, her head up. Loyse looked to the older woman as she would to a beacon of hope.

"Sigrod!"

"Aye, Lord?"

"Head south. Pick up those who come. Have them circle inland and come up behind us, so—" Simon clarified his order with gestures.

"Aye!" The Sulcarman slipped away into the broken country.

Loyse plucked at Jaelithe's mail sleeve. "Koris?" Her lips shaped that name rather than spoke it aloud.

There was a half smile on Jaelithe's face as she made answer.

"That I cannot say, little sister. That Koris' ax will swing for you—as it has swung—that is truth. But that it will do so here, that I can not tell you."

Once more a waiting. They sipped from the water container taken from the crawler, shared out mouthfuls of the dry dust which was yet food, also from the Kolder camp. And, as the sun climbed, they continued to wait. But the sun was battling clouds, and its glare did not reach into their hole to scorch them. Before midday it was blotted out entirely. Simon manned the sentry post on the crag, seeing no change below. The Kolder fortress remained sealed, the attackers waited with a super or unhuman patience in their own chosen cover.

Shortly after midday Sigrod came down through the

rocks, a tail of fighting men at his back. Mostly they were Sulcarmen, used to shore raiding, but with them also a scattering of hawk-headed helms marking Falconers, and one party of dark-featured men who came quickly to Simon, a hard core of his Borderers.

"Lord!" Ingvald lifted sword hilt in salute. He looked about him at the broken terrain. "This be a land to favor our fighting."

"Let us hope that that is so," rejoined Simon.

They held a council of war—four Sulcar captains with the pick of their fighting crews, the corps from the Borderer guard, the Falconers, so far from their own mountains but at home in this country like to those peaks. And Simon laid before them the only plan which he thought might open the Kolder keep.

"This can be done?" Captain Stymir asked, but not as if he greatly doubted the doing. Sulcar knew too much of the witches of Estcarp. Only the Falconers held aloof from magic—their avoidance of women and all the powers of women making them fear more than accept such weapons.

"We can only try," Simon replied. He looked to Jaelithe now and she gave an almost imperceptible nod.

From among the outer ranks of the men came another figure who had just caught up with the main body of the troops. As those about her she was mailed and helmed, but she also wore the gray surcoat of Estcarp and above it rested the dull gem of witchhood.

She pushed to the fore and gazed from Simon to Jaelithe and studied Jaelithe the longer.

"This you believe you can do?" she asked and Simon heard a note of derision in that inquiry.

"This we can do!" Jaelithe made a ringing promise of her answer. "We have done much else in the past days, sister."

A frown on the witch's face. Plainly she did not relish Jaelithe's title of kinship and equality. But she was willing to wait, to wait for them to fail, Simon believed. And her attitude awoke in him the same defiance, though perhaps not to a like degree, that Jaelithe's tone had made plain. Perhaps it was that defiance which gave added force to his try now.

He built up his mind-picture of the room in the keep—of the two Kolder who had faced him there. Then he narrowed that vision to the one in the cap. His will became a solid, thrusting thing, as tangible and deadly as a dart or sword blade.

That will reached out—sought—and found! His first fear was proven needless, the man of the cap lived. Alive, yes, but that which had been within him was empty—gone. Empty space could be filled for the nonce —with purpose! Simon's will entered in, and behind that flowed a vast building strength which fed and enlarged and worked at one with him—Jaelithe!

Simon was no longer aware of the rocks and the waiting men, of the witch's scornful face, even of Jaelithe, save as that other force which was also a part of him. The will ran into the emptiness of the Kolder, making him wholly theirs—as possessed as had been the slaves he and his kind had taken from Gorm, Karsten, Sulcar, all the other nations of this world they strove to bring under their rule.

Somewhere within the keep the Kolder was on the move now, answering the commands given him. A simple one to begin with: Open the close. Let in disaster. And, being no longer Kolder but possessed, he obeyed.

Simon caught hazy glimpses of that obedience—of hallways, rooms—once of a man who strove to stand between and so died. But always the obedience.

Then came a final act, a picture of a board overhung with lights, on it many controls. And the Kolder's hands moved, pressed buttons, touched levers. With his actions the defense of the keep faltered . . . died.

Then there was a sharp darkness and nothing— Simon recoiled from that nothingness, a cold terror gripping him. He was out in the open under gathering clouds, his hands clasped in Jaelithe's and the two of them staring into each other's wide eyes, the horror of that last encounter with non-being upon them both.

"He is dead." Not Jaelithe, but the witch saying that. And she was no longer aloof, but something of that terror was in her face. But her hand came up in a small salute for their sharing. "You have done as you said."

Simon moved stiff lips. "Was it enough?"

"Su!!" That cry from the spy perch. "Those demons, they are on the move!"

They were on the move, indeed. For there was a gap in the foundation of the keep, a break in the wall. And into that break streamed the skeletons from the gate world. They made no outcry, merely surged forward. Half the party were through when a shield dropped, catching two of the invaders between it and the earth in its crushing descent. These behind aimed their withering rifles at the lower edge, still kept from sealing by the bodies. And the gate shivered at that point, fell apart in jagged pieces as the rest of the skeletons beat upon it.

"Down and in!" One of the captains whirled his sword over his head, answered by the full-throated, "Su! Su!" of the raiders he commanded. The wave of the Estcarpian force flowed down the slope.

It was not pretty that taking of the heart of Kolder. And it was more a hunt than a battle. Strange weapons slew men and skeleton alike in those narrow hallways as they fought from room to room. But then those weapons failed as if the heart of Kolder missed a beat.

And, when Simon and his Borderers, together with a detachment of Falconers, fought their way into the room with the control board that heart ceased altogether. For the capped men there, six of them, died together and the great board went dead with them.

Then the second battle began, for the skeletons from

the gate turned upon the Estcarpian men. Warriors withered and died, but darts and swords could slay also.

Outside a storm raged over the barren land and inside, at last, that other and bloodier storm was stilled. Men wearied and sick of killing, men dazed from the deaths of those they held in close comrade or kinship, men unable to believe that this was the heart of Kolder and they had truly severed it with sword, dart and ax, drifted one by one into the hall where were the controls.

"Kolder is dead!" Stymir tossed his ax into the air and caught its haft, to wave it in an exultant circle. Behind him others fired as they understood what had been done this day—in spite of cruel losses.

"Kolder is dead!" Jaelithe echoed him. With the witch and Loyse she had entered the hold as part of the rearguard. "But the evil it has sown lives still. And this—perhaps others will rise to use this." She motioned to the controls.

"Not so!" The witch had taken her gem from about her throat and held it out at eye level facing the board, "Not so, sister. Let us make sure of that!"

There was a flush on Jaelithe's usually pale cheeks as she moved to stand shoulder to shoulder with the witch. Together they stared at the gem. The light in the walls had been slowly dimming, so that the chamber was dusky instead of brightly alight as it had been when they first found it.

But now there was suddenly bright sparkling on the board. Sharp explosions broke the silence. The sparks ran along the surface setting off more small explosions. A smell of burnt insulation rose in choking puffs and here and there the casing melted. Whatever energy the united power of the women released, it was fast stilling forever the controls the Kolder had used, perhaps not only to activate this hold, but to reach overseas in that web they had spun.

Simon said as much later when he waited with the captains and Ingvald for the last reports from those combing the now darkening corridors and rooms of the keep to make sure no enemy still lived.

"The web remains." The witch sat a little apart, her face drawn and haggard from her efforts to blast the controls. "And, while Kolder spun that web, the materials—the hates, the greeds, the envies from which it was fashioned—were there before they gathered them into their hands and wove them into a net to take us. Karsten is in chaos and for a space that chaos has served us, because it keeps the eyes of the great lords there from looking north, but that will not last forever."

Simon nodded. "No, it will not. Into the vacuum of no-rule will arise some leader and to him unity might come from fixing all the attention of those who would challenge him on a war beyond their borders."

Jaelithe and the witch agreed as one; Ingvald also. The Sulcar captains showed interest but not greatly so.

"And Alizon?" Loyse spoke for the first time. "How fares the war with Alizon?"

"The seneschal has raged like a moor fire into their country. He has wrought better than even we thought he might. But we cannot hold Alizon, seething with hatred for us, any more than we can take Karsten under our rule. We of Estcarp want nothing—save to be left alone in our evening. For we know it is our evening, sliding into a night for which comes no morning. But these would make that a night of flame and death and torment. No man or woman dies willingly, it is in us to strive to hold to life. Thus if we have a night of war before us—" She raised her hand and let it fall again. "Then we shall fight to the end."

"It need not be so!" There was that in Simon which refused to accept her reading of the future.

She looked from him to Jaelithe, then to Loyse, Ingvald, the Sulcar captains. Then she smiled. "I see that it is in you to will it otherwise. Well, Estcarp may go as Estcarp, but perhaps it is now a field in which we sow strange and different seed, and out of that seed may rise a new fruit. This is a time of change and the Kolder have only precipitated turmoil. Without the Kolder the elements remaining are those we have long known and so we may steady the balance for a space. At least I give you this, comrades-in-arms; this has been a quest of valor such as shall be sung by bards these thousand years until you would not know yourselves as the godlings you shall become. We shall take our victories one by one and have pride in them. And there will be no looking for the last defeat!"

"But there is an end to Kolder!" Ingvald cried out.

"An end to Kolder," Simon agreed. "There are still battles ahead, as this Wise One has said—victories to be won."

His hand went out and Jaelithe's moved to meet it. In this hour he could not visualize defeat—or night for Estcarp. Or anything—save what was his.

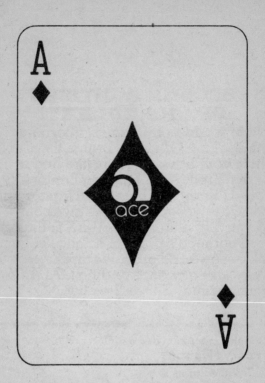

There are a lot more
where this one came from!

ORDER your FREE catalog of ACE paperbacks here. We have hundreds of inexpensive
books where this one came from priced from
75¢ to $2.50. Now you can read all the books
you have always wanted to at tremendous
savings. Order your *free* catalog of ACE
paperbacks now.

ACE BOOKS ● Box 576, Times Square Station ● New York, N.Y. 10036